A Peek Inside

"I came to say what I should've said last Sunday or last October or anytime at all. I thought I had time. I thought *we* had time. I'd intended to wait for your mourning to draw to a close, for your widow's weeds to give way to gray or purple."

Her pulse quickened. "Luke—"

He took a step closer, gestured for silence. She caught the scent of winter wind on his clothes.

"Let me finish. I don't know how to put this in words, so I'm just going to say it. This past year and a half, every time I came for you for Sunday dinner at my parents' table, every time I escorted you to Founder's Day or took you on a drive, I was just biding my time, waiting to declare myself. I'm doing that now."

Why must two men challenge her resolve at the same time? For Luke, she wanted to reconsider, and that scared her.

"Give me a chance here, Effie. I'm not asking you to marry me...yet. I intend to win your heart, bit by bit, thread by thread, until I own the masterpiece. *Then* I'll ask you to be my wife."

Praise For Maybe THIS CHRISTMAS

Well Written Clean Romance

"I loved the characters who, without exception, were honorable and of high moral standing. Oddly enough, my heart went out to Gus who was positioned as close to a villain as this possible in this story... Well done!"

~ B. D. Mann, Amazon.com, 5 stars

Exceptionally Tender Love Story

...exciting intense story. One I will read again for sure.

~ *Cinderella 7*, Amazon.com, 5 stars

I0531434

True Love Wins

She vowed to never marry again, only to have 2 men pursue her in the hopes of marrying her... lot of humor in this book.

~ *PamP.*, Amazon.com, 5 stars

Passion, Pain and Hurt

... author gives you a very interesting read so much passion, pain and hurt...

~ Cynthia, Goodreads.com, 4 stars

Luke and Effie

"You'll enjoy reading this book to find out what happens, who loves who and if love triumph over all."

~ Earline Click, Goodreads.com, 5 stars

Maybe THIS CHRISTMAS

This book is a work of fiction. Names, characters, places, and incidents are products of the writer's imagination or have been used fictitiously and are not to be construed as real. Any resemblance to persons, living or dead, actual events, business establishments, locales or organizations is entirely coincidental.

eBook and Paperback Cover designs © 2018 by Kelli Ann at Inspire Creative Services:
www.inspirecreativeservices.com

eBook and Paperback interior design by Kristin Holt:
www.KristinHolt.com

Maybe THIS CHRISTMAS

A Sweet Historical Western Holiday Romance Novella
(Rated PG)
Holidays in Mountain Home, Book 2

The books in this series are loosely connected and may be read in any order.

Luke Finlay intends to court Effie O'Leary as soon as she puts aside her widow's weeds. He's in no hurry...until August Rose, a beau from her youth, steps off the train in Mountain Home wearing a federal badge.

Effie's not sure if August—Gus—tracked her down to face criminal charges, or because he's still sweet on her. Either way, Gus's arrival causes her all sorts of grief. If Gus isn't underfoot in her tailor shop, then Luke is. It seems the two men have decided she's a prize to be won...and the escalating competition between the two leaves her torn.

She survived one disastrous marriage, so why would she accept either Gus or Luke? But these two can be most persuasive, and have a way of showing her that maybe this Christmas it's time to open her heart to love.

Sometimes even an old-fashioned courtship needs a deadline.

For my mother, a highly skilled tailor, who
learned to sew on her grandmother's treadle
machine. Thank you for patiently teaching me the
intricacies of the craft.

A Sweet Historical Western Holiday Romance
Novella (Rated PG)
Holidays in Mountain Home, Book 2

by

USA TODAY Bestselling Author

*The books in this series are loosely connected and
may be read in any order.*

To hear about New Releases, Special Sales,
and *receive a FREE novella*,
Sign up for Kristin Holt's Newsletter.

www.KristinHolt.com/newsletter

Note: Kristin is <u>e-free</u>

One

Mountain Home, Colorado
December 1899

On December first, Effie's day of reckoning arrived.

She'd known it would, eventually, so she'd savored every last day of freedom. Two years, three months, and twenty-one days.

She'd run as fast and as far as she'd known how. More than two thousand miles. It hadn't been far enough.

Late afternoon sunlight cast elongated shadows on the street beyond her shop window. Cold, gray shades of winter. In her nightmares, this scene consistently played out against brilliant colors of autumn.

He stood on the far side of the street, less than thirty feet away. With feet braced wide and fists upon narrow hips, his open greatcoat displayed a federal badge.

She hadn't seen him in five years. Dark curls hung longer than in her memory. Yet she'd know him anywhere.

An icy river flowed sluggish in her veins.

August Rose, United States Marshal.

Hunter Kendall stood at her shop's counter, admiring each piece of the infant layette he'd come for. "You outdid yourself this time, Mrs. O'Leary. Beautiful work. Miranda will be so pleased."

Effie tried to pull her panicked attention from Gus and focus on her patron. She blinked rapidly. Hunter Kendall was more than a client—he and his wife, Miranda, were her friends. *Good* friends who knew nothing of her crimes. She wished to God it were possible to bury her soiled past so deep no one in Mountain Home would hear of it.

There was no chance of that now.

Hunter refolded a baby gown made of the finest cotton. "Miranda's anxious for the little one to come."

He seemed to want a response, so Effie made a sympathetic sound. Her throat had constricted, her thoughts scattered to the four winds. She could do no better.

"We're staying at the Finlays' through New Year's, maybe longer."

Of course she'd want to be with her mother, though her own home was a scant mile away.

"Wish her well for me, won't you?" How could her voice sound natural?

A four-horse team pulled a heavily loaded wagon past, blocking her view of Gus. Time slowed like molasses poured in January. Her breathing rasped too loud as her fear doubled.

"Sure will." Hunter ambled to the shelves lining the north wall. His gaze roved over the display of fabrics and he paused to finger a cotton flannel in pale buttercup. "This is nice."

The wagon finally cleared. Gus strode straight for her door.

Her heart skipped two beats and slammed back into rhythm.

"Is this spoken for?" Hunter was oblivious to her distress. "I picture a night dress and wrapper. A timely Christmas present for my wife, don't you think? I want to give her something that makes her feel beautiful, especially after the baby comes."

Effie gripped the wooden counter top, panic rooting her boots to the floor.

Run!

The back door. She could make it that far—but he would apprehend her within seconds.

Hunter seemed to really see her then. "Mrs. O'Leary?"

She blinked, desperate to mask her terror. If Hunter read her, he'd stay and try to help.

Gus no doubt brought proof of her true identity, along with a warrant for her arrest.

Hunter, bless his good-hearted soul, took a step closer. "You feeling all right, ma'am?"

Bells hanging from the doorknob clattered as Gus pushed the door open. Winter air swirled in, but Effie was already too cold. She fought to keep her focus on Hunter...and failed.

Don't let it be him. Please, let it be a trick of the light, a waking nightmare...

His gray eyes zeroed in on her, pinned her to the spot.

Definitely Gus Rose.

Her stomach rolled all the way over within her too-tight corset.

Hunter followed her gaze over his shoulder. He glanced at the newcomer long enough to make a decision. He covered one of her clenched hands, a soothing touch meant to convey...something. Support? Kindness? He raised one brow as if to repeat his question: *You feeling all right?*

She needed Hunter to leave. *Now.*

She didn't want *anyone* to witness her humiliation. If anyone overheard the conversation sure to come, the sensational news would spread. By the time Gus forced her onto tomorrow's train in shackles, everyone would know.

Hunter leaned both elbows on the counter, as if he had all the time in the world. "Think you've got time to squeeze that project in before Christmas? I'll pay double your rate." His smile said what words did not—he'd look out for her until the stranger was long gone.

For once, she wished her friend's husband wasn't so kind.

Effie cleared her throat, fought for breath. With trembling hands she pulled out her ledger and scanned the entries, unable to make sense of it. "Yes. For you, yes." If, by some miracle she were still here, she'd do it.

"Put it down, then. Can't have that beautiful cloth going to anyone else now, can I?" He claimed the yardage off the shelf and set it on the counter. He'd been in often enough to know Effie set aside fabric once selected. "I'm thinking a long row of buttons down the front, to make it easy with the baby."

"Yes, of course." She tried to smile, quite impossible with Gus watching her every move.

"Long sleeves, high neck. Tucks at the shoulders?"

Fortunately, Gus remained in her line of sight, leaning against the door frame. A smile of triumph curved his mouth—a cat who'd cornered his prey, content to toy with it.

Passersby bundled against the winter cold paused to admire the display she'd put in the window last night. Two more customers stopped. *Move along, keep going.*

Gus drew her attention, his smile now more amusement than triumph. She recognized his compassion in allowing her to finish with her customer...an unexpected kindness.

"You have her measurements?" Hunter asked.

She nodded, smiled as genuinely as she could muster, praying he wouldn't detest her when he heard the sordid details.

Hunter Kendall was a good man—a rare breed. He and Miranda had been blissfully happy together. Effie had never known contentment—

much less love like theirs—in her ill-fated marriage. Which led her to this fate.

Quickly, she documented Hunter's order in the ledger, wrapped the baby's layette in brown paper and tied it with string. He paid in full with a generous tip, despite her protestations.

"Thank you, Mr. Kendall." She tried to convey far more than appreciation for his patronage. "Give Miranda my best? Kiss the baby for me."

"You'll come visit after the birth, won't you? Surely you can get away on a Sunday afternoon."

The shop was closed on Sundays, and she'd made a habit of visiting friends. She'd miss it. She'd miss everything about Mountain Home. She nodded.

The weight of all she would lose provoked tears. She would *not* cry, she would *not* plead. She'd made her bed, and she'd lie in it.

"On second thought—" Hunter dug deep into his pocket. "Let me leave a deposit on the night clothes." He quickly counted a few coins and set them on the counter. "We'll settle when I pick it up. Or you can send it with Noelle."

Miranda's younger sister Noelle worked three days a week as Effie's assistant. Thank goodness the young woman wasn't here to witness her humiliation.

"Yes. Th-thank you." Anxiety flushed her body hot and cold all at once. With Hunter's departure, nothing stood between the pretense of normality and incarceration.

Hunter pulled on his gloves, nodded to Gus,

and with the layette bundle beneath his arm, left the shop.

Cold air swirled about Effie's ankles, swishing the hem of her widow's weeds.

The bells hanging from the knob tinkled. The door had barely shut when Gus flipped the sign to *CLOSED*. He pulled down the rolling shade over the front door's window.

Her heart raced.

Too bad the bay window didn't have privacy shades because several curious faces peered in. *No, no! Must* Hunter join the crowd at her window?

Within the quarter-hour, everyone in Mountain Home would know of her disgrace. Gut-twisting agony made her weak-kneed. So many friends and neighbors trusted her. Numerous orders were half-completed, and she'd accepted payment on dozens not yet delivered. They'd be justifiably angry over the loss of hard-earned money.

Her thoughts raced ahead—she'd leave instructions with Mr. McGillicudy at the bank to issue refunds—

Gus twisted the key in the lock. The soft click thrust her heart into a frantic staccato.

She expected him to pocket the key but he left it in the keyhole. Armed, twice her weight, a predator—she couldn't escape him and he knew it.

Bile rose in her throat and she feared she'd be sick.

His boots thumped ominously on the polished floorboards.

She fell back a step. All determination to accept her fate fled like the wind. "G-Gus, listen, please. I can explain—"

Two steps closer. His feral grin widened.

Her back collided with the back wall. "I know it wasn't right..."

If he had an ounce of compassion, if he recalled the tender feelings they'd once had—

He snagged her wrist.

—for each other, he *wouldn't* do this!

She expected the cold slap of iron.

Instead, he yanked her arm, tipping her off balance. She fell against his chest and found herself looking up...way up...into eyes the color of a storm-tossed Atlantic.

"If you knew *why* I did—"

In that split second, she glimpsed the intention in his eyes—what? Surely he didn't mean to—

Her breath snagged in her throat.

He lowered his head and claimed her mouth with a kiss.

Luke pitched hay off the feed wagon. He'd stripped down to shirtsleeves as the hot, sweaty work soaked him through. He welcomed the cold wind.

Timothy drove the wagon at the pace of a man's walk, and Dallas pitched hay beside him. The cattle meandered in from the wide expanse of snow-covered pasture where foraging had grown significantly difficult as the past week's snowstorm buried dormant vegetation.

Beyond the fence, he caught a glimpse of Hunter returning on his sorrel.

Hunter dropped the reins, tossed a paper-wrapped package onto the front porch, and ran toward the pasture. He vaulted the fence and sank into a snowdrift.

"Halt," Luke called to Tim. "Something's wrong." Hunter always checked on Miranda *first*.

He leapt from the wagon and met his brother-in-law halfway.

Hunter cupped a hand about his mouth while a good thirty feet out. "Trouble."

"What?" Luke charged the last few steps, nudging aside milling cattle, nearly losing a boot in snow packed by the repeated passage of the feed wagon and hundreds of hooves. "What happened?"

"A newcomer in town. A stranger." Hunter breathed hard from exertion. How fast had he ridden on icy roads?

Awareness prickled his nape.

"It's better you hear this from me, from family." Hunter paused, stretching a beat too long for Luke's comfort. "And not the rumor mill."

"Spit it out."

"This newcomer got off the four-o'clock and headed straight to Pettingill's."

Dread curdled in Luke's gut. "What does he want with Effie?" He trusted his brother-in-law to act in widowed Mrs. O'Leary's defense or at *least* fetch the sheriff.

"He kissed her."

The news landed like a slap across his cheek. "He *what?*"

"He waited until I left the shop, as patient as could be. I watched through the display window alongside a half-dozen others. The fellow backed her up against the rear wall and kissed her."

"A peck?" Some people kissed a cheek in greeting, like maybe...a brother?

Hunter shook his head. "Full on the mouth."

No one should kiss Widow O'Leary but *him*. Just 'cause he hadn't actually kissed her, *yet*, didn't mean he didn't want to.

"It's time to act...if you're going to."

The yank on the conversation's reins caught Luke unprepared. He hadn't told a soul, certainly not Hunter, that he was sweet on Mrs. O'Leary.

"I speak from experience." Hunter glanced toward the feed wagon and back. "Don't let her get away without a fight. It's time she knows your intentions."

Luke's stomach curdled. *He backed her up against the rear wall of the shop and kissed her. Full on the mouth.*

It's too late.

The slow, not-yet-official courtship— escorting Mrs. O'Leary to the church picnic, occasionally bringing her home to enjoy a Sunday dinner with his boisterous family, oiling hinges on her shop's door—hadn't been enough.

Effie O'Leary had no idea Luke Finlay courted

her with an eye toward marriage.

Until this moment, he'd wanted it that way.

He'd thought to allow her time to grieve her lost husband, to put aside her widow's weeds of her own accord before stating his intentions. He'd gradually worked toward a full-fledged courtship, believing he had ample time to win her affections.

And now a *stranger* had stepped off the four-o'clock and interrupted Luke's courtship of Effie before it could officially begin.

Of all the rotten luck.

He clenched his jaw against the urge to swear long and hard.

"Why are you standing here? *Go.*"

Luke turned to his younger brothers, standing on the feed wagon. "Finish dropping the hay," he bellowed, "I'm going to town."

Hunter clapped him on the shoulder. "Better take a quick bath if you're going courting."

Luke glared at his beloved brother-in-law, knowing full well he smelled of hay and sweat and horse. "I know all about courting."

Hunter's features fell slack in mock surprise. "You do?"

Luke refused to rise to the bait. He kept the tone serious. "Thanks for bringing word."

"Anytime."

"And I'll thank you," Luke said, holding Hunter's gaze, "to keep your suppositions to yourself."

"About Effie O'Leary and you?"

"Yes."

"Everyone already knows—except her, but I'll keep it to myself just the same. Better get on into town before he kisses her again." Hunter chuckled. "Or drags her in front of Reverend Gilbert."

Two

It was full dark by the time Luke reached the outskirts of Mountain Home proper. Moonlight reflected off drifted snow, illuminating the terrain. His breath showed in puffs of white.

He nudged Domino down the frozen, muddy street to Pettingill's. Light streamed through the windows. Luke had no intention of losing Mrs. Effie O'Leary to *anyone*.

He dismounted and tossed the reins over the hitching post. He patted Domino's spotted neck and stepped onto the boardwalk. He stomped off the slush and mud, mindful of Effie's shining floors.

No small crowd had gathered to peer in her windows at the two wire dress forms proudly displaying a woman's woolen suit in brown, trimmed with black piping and matching buttons. The dapper style looked just like an image in her New York catalog. The second form presented a man's three-piece suit, fit for Sundays or a prosperous businessman. A little dashing for a rancher like him, but someone in town would look mighty fine.

Mrs. O'Leary had a gift for tailoring.

Gifted or not, Christmas season or not, *far too many* customers crowded her shop. Luke entered, setting the bells to jingling.

Nearly a dozen shoppers browsed the various fabrics lining the shelves and gathered in knots of two or three, their heads close together in whispered conversation. Others lined up at the counter, evidently to place orders. But Luke caught tidbits of conversation and realized these ladies congregated under the pretense of looking over newly delivered fabric and placing yet another Christmas order...but they were obviously here for *details*.

They'd heard all about a stranger, *tall, impossibly handsome, dark*—if the murmurs could be believed—and his most familiar and romantic kiss. They wanted to know more.

He didn't like it, but understood their need for information.

He scanned the shop for this mysterious, tall, and handsome stranger. No one fit the bill. *Good.*

Behind the counter, Effie had a pen poised above her ledger, prepared to jot down Mrs. Whipple's order. Every glossy blond hair was in place, but her posture seemed stiff and her trademark dimpled smile conspicuously absent. Her hand shook as she wrote, and worse, she trembled like an autumn leaf in the wind.

Must've been *some* kiss.

Pain shot through Luke's jaw. He'd clenched his teeth—again. He shook it off, determined to *do* something, step in, create order from chaos, and help with Effie's crush of customers. If he'd already declared himself, he might have put two fingers in his mouth, whistle long and hard, and order everybody out.

For all he knew, Effie wanted every last penny these shoppers would spend in their quest for gossip. She wouldn't appreciate him herding her paying customers out the door.

So he assessed what he *could* do.

With all the comings and goings, the door was open more than it was shut, so he headed to the potbellied stove. He eased between clusters of ladies, murmuring apologies, and checked the fire. He fed it two logs, latched the door, and pulled off his coat.

Just as he hung it on a peg, the shop's door opened and a man came inside with a rush of frigid air.

The chattering ladies quieted one by one. Every last eye seemed to turn toward this unknown man...the stranger who'd swept in on the four o'clock and kissed Effie.

Luke's trusted brother-in-law had seen it with his own two eyes. This wasn't hearsay. Thinking about it curdled Luke's easy-going nature. He straightened—no sense slouching when sizing up the competition.

The stranger was, indeed, tall. Luke grudgingly admitted that to *some* women, he might be considered handsome with dark hair curling nearly to his shoulders and a well-trimmed beard fringing a prominent jaw. Luke disliked him on sight. Or on principle. Or both.

"Evening, Ladies." The man greeted the crowd as he kicked the door shut. He balanced two covered plates on gloved hands. "It's dinnertime for Mrs. O'Leary. You won't mind if we close up shop now, do you? Come back tomorrow."

Luke shot a glance at Mrs. O'Leary. Did she want this stranger ordering everyone around, sending her clientele away, and...and *feeding* her?

Her trembling worsened and she fumbled the ink bottle. She seemed both unwilling to look in the stranger's direction and unable to pull her attention away. This was not the Effie he knew and adored, a woman who spoke her mind and stood up for herself. This stranger made her anxious, wary, and...afraid.

That got Luke's goat. Couldn't anyone else see how this man...this *interloper*...affected Effie?

Now he didn't merely dislike the other guy— he had good reason to distrust him.

Luke bit back a growl. He'd ridden five miles on a bitter winter night to say what he needed to say, and by golly, he would say it before he turned tail and went back home. Right after he dispatched

Mr. Interloper.

He waited for the tittering and skirt-swirling ladies to head on out the door.

He knew the embroidered pale blue towels and fancy dishes Mr. Interloper set on the counter. He peeled off his gloves and coat, and tossed them on the end of the counter top.

Luke caught sight of a emblem pinned on the vest. *U.S. Marshal.* Nothing to get excited about.

Pistols rode at each hip in a finely tooled holster. He wore citified clothes that must've been tailored with only him in mind. Lean, brawny, broad, and hard.

A formidable opponent.

Who *was* he?

Luke rather liked that the stranger was on the customer side of the counter, while he stood behind the long bar with Effie. He took his place at her side. A simple message that didn't need words: *I stand with Mrs. O'Leary and you don't belong here.*

"Evening." The man offered a big hand in greeting.

After a hesitation, Luke accepted. "Evening." He squeezed just enough to show he wasn't put off by the badge. He'd wrangled cattle since he could walk and figured he could toss this fellow, if need be.

"August Rose."

August Rose? What kind of a name was that? His parents must not have liked him much.

Neither name nor badge answered the

burning question—*what* was this guy, to Effie?

August Rose's grip was firm and nearly joint-cracking. "You are...?"

"Luke Finlay." He withdrew and casually put his arm about Effie. He felt her trembling and gave her a little squeeze for strength. If Rose couldn't see how edgy he made Effie, he must be blind.

"Well, Mr. Finlay, it's a pleasure, but you'd best be going," Rose said. "Our supper's getting cold."

"Go ahead and eat. I'll stay."

Rose shrugged. "I brought only enough for two."

"Don't mind me. I didn't come for supper."

Luke held Rose's gaze, irritated by the condescension he glimpsed in the competition's eye.

"Suit yourself." Rose came around the counter, took a plate in one hand and Effie's elbow in the other.

Luke let her go, but he didn't like it.

He watched as Rose ushered her to a chair in the corner where Noelle often sat to ply a needle in finish work. Once Effie sat, he handed her a plate and fork.

Rose claimed his dinner plate, leaned against the counter, and crossed one boot over the other. He dug into fragrant roast beef, boiled potatoes drenched in gravy, roasted carrots with butter and herbs, and a golden roll.

Luke's empty stomach rumbled. If he'd stayed home, he'd have joined the family at the table long before now. He crossed his arms and willed his stomach to quiet down. He caught himself grinding his molars and forced his jaw to relax—this confrontation wasn't worth a trip to the tooth-puller.

He waited. Ranching had taught him a good deal of patience.

Rose had consumed half his meal while Effie picked at hers. She may have taken a bite of two but it was hard to tell if she actually ate anything. This wasn't the happy, joyful, confident woman who relished a home-cooked meal at his mother's table. He'd seen her eat plenty of times...she wasn't eating now. She seemed frail, fragile, like a stiff wind would knock her over.

Time to see August Rose to the door. "You're passing through town, I see."

"No." Rose dredged his roll through gravy. "I've come to take Effie home. With me." He popped the rest of the roll in his mouth and grinned.

Effie's throat closed.

I've come to take Effie home...with me.

In chains? To stand trial?

Since Gus's threatening arrival, this was the first time they were alone...or nearly alone. Those gathered outside her shop's window had witnessed that shocking kiss and applauded with vigor. The commotion had distracted Gus, so she'd wriggled free and unlocked the door. He'd erred in admitting he wouldn't handcuff her before an audience.

The bells on her door kept tinkling and the precious audience grew...and brought dozens of questions and abundant curiosity. They'd wanted to see this stranger for themselves.

Exhaustion caught up with her. Constant fretting wore her so thin she feared the fabric of her being would split at the seams. She *needed* to know why he'd come...and what prompted his unwelcome kiss.

She squeezed her eyes shut against a resurgence of panic. The scuttle of wind against the frame building and scrape of Gus's utensil upon china chafed her raw nerves. Her dull headache flared hot.

Luke must leave. She needed privacy to demand answers of Gus.

Mere seconds had passed since Gus's statement—he intended to take her home—it seemed an eternity.

Luke shifted his weight. A floorboard squeaked beneath him. "Is that right."

"Yes." Another scrape of fork against china.

"I don't like," Luke stated, "the temperament you bring out in Mrs. O'Leary."

Gus chuckled.

Don't ask, Luke. Don't.

"You frighten her and I don't like it. Who are you, exactly?" Tension coiled in Luke's thick shoulders.

"Just who I said. August Rose."

"A United States Marshal."

Gus held Luke's gaze and finally nodded. "Yes."

"Just as *I* said, I don't like the temperament you bring out in Mrs. O'Leary."

Why must he choose *now*, of all moments, to nominate himself her protector? She needed him gone before he learned too much. She swallowed to moisten her mouth. "It's okay, Luke. I'm okay. I'm simply tired."

Luke kept his attention on Gus and barely acknowledged she'd spoken. "Why, exactly, are you here? What do you want?"

"An old friend," she blurted. "He's an old friend."

Luke studied her, taking in far more, she feared, than she wanted to disclose. Then to Gus, "What kind of old friend?"

Gus folded his arms, leaned a hip against the counter. "Why, the kind of old friend she's happy to see."

"Doesn't look that way to me."

Effie split a glance between the two men. Luke's jaw set like granite. Gus's eyes darkened.

"I'm just tired." *Go, please. Leave.* "It's been a very trying day."

She stood and set her dinner plate on the cutting table.

Luke held her gaze, and she fancied she glimpsed more than neighborly protectiveness. His concern felt wonderful...and undeserved.

"You want him to go?" Luke gestured to Gus with a nudge of his jaw.

If she said yes, Gus would morph into August Rose, U.S. Marshal. "No. I'm sorry, Luke. I need *you* to go. Gus and I have matters to discuss."

Disappointment and confusion marred his handsome features. "If that's what you want."

Gus tossed the towel over his empty plate and waited in expectant silence.

She willed Luke to understand. "It is what I want."

Yet there was no way he could understand—but he would. By tomorrow night, the gossip would reach every ear in town and every soul in the valley by week's end. He'd hear all about it soon enough.

This was goodbye.

She reached for his hand.

He accepted the invitation, his large, warm, callused fingers closing about hers. Distrust of Gus registered plainly on his face...and deep hurt. He didn't understand.

Anguish squeezed her throat. How it hurt to see the pain she'd caused.

She swallowed hard. "Thanks, Luke." *Thanks for the friendship, companionship, and laughter. Thanks for trying to help me.*

She'd miss him.

He released her, shrugged on his coat, buttoned up and pulled on gloves. Raw injury darkened his expression and his pain became her own.

She hated herself for hurting him, sending

him away when he clearly wanted to support and protect.

From this, from her own doing, Luke could not save her. No one could.

He strode for the door and jerked it open.

She expected him to slam the door, and braced for it. With complete and utter calm, he closed the door.

He did not look back. A rush of white-hot pain seared through her heart.

Gus turned the key in the lock. "Let's find ourselves some privacy, away from prying eyes." He put out two of the three burning lamps.

She nodded in mute acceptance.

He carried the last lamp to the rear of the shop and opened the door to her private room. He held the light high as if expecting a crowded storage space. The room ran the width of the shop, but had a depth of only seven feet. The headboard of a narrow bed resided in the corner furthest from the door, and one trunk in the nearby corner. One bedside table, one chair, and pegs on the wall for her clothing. A door, flanked by a single window, led out back to the necessary.

The room was significantly colder, without stove or hearth. Gus set the lamp on the table.

He remained standing, so she did, too. "Tell me what you meant."

"Meant by what?"

"You said you're here to take me home. With you." The words tumbled free, rushed and panicked. She hated feeling so unsettled, so trapped...so like...*before.*

"I meant exactly what I said. I'm here to take you home with me." He gripped her shoulders in unyielding hands. "It's time to come home." A smile formed on his lips, as if he believed everything would be okay.

Nothing could be okay, would *never* be okay again. "Am I under arrest?"

"Arrest? *No.*"

"I can explain. I *want* to explain."

"Effie, listen. He's gone—"

"Who's gone?"

He chuckled. "You're just as impatient as always." Without warning, he gathered her close. "I missed you."

His embrace seemed both suffocating and oh, so wonderful. How long had it been since a man had hugged her with joyful affection? She squirmed.

He didn't release her. "Reuben Carmichael is dead."

She stilled and closed her eyes, grateful Gus couldn't see her expression. Oh, yes, she most certainly had known he was dead—she'd been there.

His big hand swept up her back and cradled her neck. "It's okay. It's all okay."

"It's *not* okay." Breathless, she tried to draw in air. "I must explain." Panic flared, this time because she couldn't breathe. "If you have an ounce," she panted, "of affection left. *Listen.* And *help* me."

Gus eased back and searched her gaze in the lamplight. "I'll listen, but you need to know Carmichael died eleven months ago. Snug in his bed. Pneumonia."

Her knees nearly buckled. *Eleven months ago.* When she'd been long gone and safely disguised as Widow O'Leary.

With blood rushing through her ears, her heart pounding, she wasn't sure she'd heard right. "Eleven months? You're sure?"

"Positive. It was in the papers. I personally saw his body lying in repose at the mansion."

She'd run, knowing it didn't matter one whit whether she'd actually killed Reuben or simply injured him gravely. There had been *so* much blood. If he'd recovered, he'd want vengeance...if dead, his brother would've seen her prosecuted.

The scents of wind and snow, tobacco and man clung to him, achingly familiar and yet new.

He nudged her chin up. "I've searched for you ever since. You hid real well, Effie. It took me longer to find you than I'd thought possible."

"Why?"

He smiled, his visage softening, offering a glimpse of the young man he'd once been. "I'm usually a better tracker than that."

"No—why search for me at all? Are you here to arrest me? You're taking me back to stand trial?"

"No." The gray of his eyes clouded over, softened with unmistakable compassion. He cupped her face between hands at once familiar and yet bigger, rougher, stronger. "I had to find you. To tell you you're free."

She'd never be free of the past. The Carmichaels wouldn't allow it.

"You know why I left." Everyone in law enforcement no doubt knew. Reuben and his family would've seen to that.

"I know enough."

"They won't rest. If I return, if I'm anywhere near, they'll see me punished."

"I doubt that."

He didn't know the Carmichaels. "Reuben's brother is as influential as he is—*was*. He'll never forgive bludgeoning his brother with leaded crystal."

So slowly, Gus lowered his head, telegraphing his intention to kiss her again. Had he heard a word she'd said?

She had ample time to turn away, deny him, deny herself. He paused halfway, his attention sliding from her mouth to her eyes as if asking permission. He must've seen a *yes* there, for his lips touched hers in a gentle kiss, sweet and welcoming, reminded her of forbidden kisses in the first blush of adulthood.

The play of his lips upon hers allowed a glimpse of the youth within the mature lawman. Her heart rolled over—how she'd loved him, once.

"I've come to take you home." His tone left no room for argument. "It's time. Without Carmichael and your father keeping us apart, you're finally mine."

"My father?" Her heart pounded and her ears

rang. "What do you mean, without my father?"

Her father had successfully interrupted the only joy in her life...her romance with Gus. He'd chosen Reuben Carmichael because of his position as federal judge. He'd sold her into slavery to purchase security for his unlawful business empire.

Gus soothed her with a touch. "He's dead. And your mother."

Dead? The news rendered her incapable of speech.

They'd been very much alive when she'd fled Hartford. If she'd approached them for help, they'd have returned her to her husband. So she'd left Hartford without contacting her parents.

Only one regret haunted her still—she'd also severed ties with was her only sibling, Victoria.

"You didn't know."

She shook her head.

"The papers reported your father passed after a brief illness. I did some digging." He shrugged. "Natural causes. His heart, most likely. Consumption claimed your mother a few months later."

"Tori." What had become of her little sister? Did the sweet, quiet girl with luminous eyes believe Effie dead? What purgatory had Father consigned her to?

"She's well. Lives in the family home, fights with your father's lawyers, and typically wins. She'll be happy I've found you." Gus grinned. "She hired me to find you."

Three

The following morning, Effie stretched within the warm cocoon of her bed.

The barrage of information—the death of her parents and the death of her estranged husband, word of her sister...it had all been too much. She'd needed time.

Somewhere in the middle of the night, she'd realized she'd never set Gus straight.

He'd kissed her, implied he loved her still. He wanted to take her home with him.

She would not go. Honestly, the Carmichaels had very little to do with her decision. She would not go because Gus expected marriage.

She'd learned the hard way marriage was not

for her. Never again would she give a man control over every aspect of her life.

Never.

She and Gus wanted two very different things, thus they had no hope of a future together. She couldn't allow him to make further plans, to assume she'd do as he bid. Yes, she'd wanted to marry him, once, but that had been a very long time ago. Before she learned what marriage was truly like.

She'd ensure he understood, at the first opportunity.

She stretched, basking in the excellent news Gus had delivered.

I'm free.

Free of Reuben Carmichael's threats, free of his moneyed long-arm reach, free of marriage, free of her parents' manipulations.

Free.

She could stay here in Mountain Home, continue operating her business. She'd be around to sew the flannel nightgown and wrapper Hunter ordered as a Christmas present for his wife. She would hold her friends' baby.

Relief swelled, an unfamiliar emotion she didn't know what to do with.

She tossed back the covers, pushed her toes into chilly slippers and reached for her wrapper. Morning's light eased from grays to muted shades of color.

Happy anticipation fueled her desire to dive into her work. Within thirty minutes, she'd stoked the fire, heated water for a sponge bath, dressed, twisted her hair into a knot atop her head, made her bed, and brewed coffee. She briskly swept the floor to remove the dirt tracked in last night by curious folk.

She'd nearly finished the job when a light tap sounded on her front window. She glanced up to find Gus back-lit by early dawn. He waved to her.

"What are you doing out so early?"

He brought a rush of bitter cold air with him inside. He stomped clumps of snow off his boots and leaned on the door to shut it.

So much for swept floors.

"I couldn't wait to see you." A grin softened his features.

"I'm glad you're here." She'd rather set him straight in private.

"Good." He leaned in, expecting a kiss.

She gave him her cheek. "I've carefully thought through everything you told me last night."

"Anxious to go home?"

"Actually, no."

He paused in the process of shedding his heavy coat. "No need to worry over the Carmichaels. I know you've been in hiding from them—I understand. They searched for you after your abrupt departure, but quickly turned their story into a tale that favored the family."

She could imagine what they'd said. Likely that she'd left to visit a distant relative. Or that she'd been confined to her bed with consumption.

Certainly not that she'd left Reuben Carmichael and disappeared. Never that.

Gus removed heavy leather gloves, then pulled something from his coat pocket. He presented stiff papers with a flourish.

"What's this?" But she already knew. Railway tickets.

"I bought two return fares. One for you. One for me."

Her heart sank. Rather presumptuous of him, wasn't it?

She must've given away her displeasure for he rushed to continue, "You'll be home in time for Christmas. Think of it. Christmas in Hartford, with Tori."

Tempting, but inadequate. "Thank you, Gus, for your generosity. I need you to understand—"

"I'll help you pack. We can make the four-o'clock."

"No, thank you."

"It's too big a job to do alone."

"No. I mean, thank you, but I won't pack. I won't leave today."

He paused, his expression slack with disbelief. He glanced about the shop, taking in the value of her inventory, her sewing machine, seemed to recognize she had a business to operate. "I guess you need time to sell the place. I'll help. We'll get word out—"

"I intend to stay."

"You *can't* be serious."

She'd spent too many years under Reuben's

control, cowering beneath his temper. She intentionally straightened her posture. Gus wasn't anything like her disastrous husband—she hoped. "This is my home. This is *my* business." It represented independence and safety.

"I love you." His deep baritone constricted with emotion. "I've loved you since I was fifteen years old." His features contorted.

It seemed too cruel to tell him she didn't love him anymore, hadn't loved him for a very long time. After a pledge like this, what was the best way to inform him of her iron-clad decision to remain unmarried?

"I had no way to claim you, not before. Not when your father wielded the power, not when he'd already contracted with Carmichael." His wide, strong shoulders slumped."I loved you every last day you were wed to that pompous fool, Euphemia Scofield. I loved you enough to search for you for nearly a year. I love you enough to take you home with me, keep you safe. We'll marry in Hartford, in front of the whole world, with your sister standing up with you."

Did he realize he hadn't asked her opinion nor considered her wishes? "It sounds lovely, but—"

"*We,*" Gus informed her, "are leaving no later than day after tomorrow. And we're getting married no later than New Year's."

"No. We're not."

He stared at her as if he could not reconcile her answer with the truth according to August

Rose.

"I'm flattered, honored that you want me for your wife after all this time. But you must listen to me. I've made up my mind. I will never again marry."

"Carmichael."

That's all he need say. He did understand, at least a little. "Yes, my marriage was an unmitigated disaster. I learned far too much about the consequences of turning over every ounce of control to a man." Old, once-buried desperation and fear resurfaced, sitting on her chest with the weight of a full-grown man. She couldn't breathe.

"I'm not Reuben Carmichael."

She raised a hand, indicated she understood that to be true. She fought for breath, reminded herself she'd left that oppression behind.

When she regained her composure, she continued, feeling she owed Gus more of an explanation. "I don't like the woman I became, what marriage did to me. I chafed in the confines of marriage. I won't go through that again."

"That was an arranged marriage, you didn't choose him..." He paused. "It will be different— good—with you and me."

"You can't promise that. *I'm* not cut out for marriage. I would make any man a poor wife."

"I can't accept that. You and I would've been happy, had we eloped like we wanted to."

No matter what angle he argued, she wouldn't change her mind. "I *need* my independence. I choose to remain unwed."

He shook his head, as if he'd never considered the possibility of rejection. "I pursued employment with the Marshals to get close to you."

That gave her pause. She'd seen the notice in the paper the day Gus was first sworn in. He'd been the youngest man given that honor in Hartford's history.

"U.S. Marshals were assigned to guard Reuben Carmichael. If I had that job, I could get myself assigned to him. I'd be nearer to you."

Her heart pounded, but she knew he wasn't a deranged man, unable to accept the loss of a would-be bride. No. He had risen in the ranks, gone after what he wanted and claimed it. No apologies, no time wasted. The man exercised patience and confidence.

And he wanted her.

The realization was both flattering and terrifying.

"Please, don't turn this into a contest of wills. You and I want significantly different things. We are at cross-purposes and cannot both win."

He gathered his coat and slowly donned it. He buttoned from the collar on down. "You've spoken your mind, and I heard every word. It seems you heard me out, too."

She nodded, relief somehow compounding the deep sadness aching at the pit of her stomach. It hurt to say goodbye. "Thank you for bringing me word of...of Carmichael. And of my parents."

He nodded. A long moment passed and he made no further conversation nor move toward the door.

"Thank you for searching for me." *Thank you for respecting my decision.*

"It sounds like you're saying goodbye." A hint of a smile toyed with his full lips.

She smiled, just a little. "I guess I am." Surely he'd take his train tickets and be on today's four-o'clock.

He eased on one glove, then the other. "Well, that's where you're mistaken. I've a mind to stay in Mountain Home for awhile, enjoy the fresh mountain air, and spend time with you."

Oh, *no.*

"After all," he murmured, "you and I are were good friends once. You loved me, then, and I believe you'll come to love me again." He winked and smiled broadly.

The bells tinkled as he shut the door behind himself.

Effie stumbled toward the chair in the back corner and sat, and dropped her head between her knees. *Breathe. Just breathe.*

She'd made up her mind. She would *not* soften, would not reconsider, would *never* marry again—no matter how long Gus remained in Mountain Home.

Luke boarded Domino at the livery across the street from Effie's shop. He didn't know how long he'd be, and he couldn't leave the gelding standing in the frigid wind.

First hints of daylight shaded the eastern sky in pinks and purples. It was far too early to pay a social call, except in the most dire of circumstances.

This qualified.

Last night, he'd watched her through the shop's front window from a shadowed alley. He'd seen the marshal take her into the back room. Though he'd wanted to pound on the door and insist they do their talking in plain sight of the street, he'd waited until Rose finally quit Pettingill's for the boardinghouse. He'd waited a half-hour more, 'til he could reasonably believe Rose was in for the night.

By the time Luke had saddled up and headed home, he'd had ice in his bones.

This morning, Effie's demeanor still haunted him. She'd sent him away last night, and he'd gone, out of some misguided respect for her wishes. Not this time. They were going to have a talk, and he wouldn't leave until he understood the threat August Rose posed.

As he left the livery and stepped into the frozen mud of the street, the door of Pettingill's opened and shut. *August Rose.*

What was he doing here at this hour?

The marshal struck a match and cupped his hands around the flame, but it would take a whole lot more than that to hide his scowl. He drew deeply on the cigarette and exhaled smoke.

Luke halted, one boot on the boardwalk at his

back, and one on the street. By the looks of August's departure, he wasn't happy.

That made two of them.

The lawman bent into the wind and headed to Ihnken's Boardinghouse. He'd better stay there. Luke was in no mood to mind his manners or keep his fists to himself.

"Come in out of the cold." Effie must've seen him coming because she met him at the door. Her dimpled smile faltered. "What's wrong? Is it Miranda?"

"No, she's fine." The shop was toasty warm and smelled of fresh coffee. "I'm here about you."

"Me?" She gestured him nearer to the stove's heat.

"Yes, you. I saw how Rose affected you last night—I've never seen you that anxious—and you sent me away. I'm back to check on you."

She merely nodded as if resigned. Color had returned to her cheeks and the shakes had stopped.

It wasn't enough. "I saw him leaving just now. Is he bothering you?"

"No."

He took notice of a pair of train tickets weighted with dressmaker shears.

She noticed where his attention had gone. "I told him no. I won't go."

He figured he understood why. She operated a successful business and had the freedom to do as she pleased. The folks of Mountain Home liked and respected her, considered her one of their own.

"You won't go where?"

"Home...Connecticut."

Luke had taken a hard look at the U.S. Marshal angle during the night. He'd seen the way Rose looked at Effie, with a certainty and propriety Luke hadn't appreciated. Despite the badge, it looked personal. He didn't know what to make of it. "Why? Official business, or something personal?"

"He offered to take me back home. I have a sister. He thought..."

He could well imagine what August Rose thought. His mood darkened further. He noticed Effie hadn't actually answered his question.

"You want to stay here, despite the chance to visit your sister?"

"We were never close." She sighed. "This is my home."

"Good. It's settled."

She nodded.

He claimed the two unwanted tickets from beneath her scissors and prepared to return them to their owner.

"I know you, Mrs. O'Leary, and an old friend showing up, offering to accompany you to visit a sister isn't nearly enough to ruffle your feathers this much. Something else is wrong."

Her gaze flitted about landing everywhere but on him.

"I can't defend you, protect you properly, if I don't know what I'm up against. It's obvious you're in trouble. Let me help." He searched her gaze but found no answers there. "Tell me the truth. Trust me."

"It's not like that. He just brought news." Her gaze skittered away. "My—" She paused, drew a deep breath, let it out with agonizing slowness. "My parents have passed away...he simply thought to deliver the news."

"I'm sorry to hear your parents are gone, Effie...but he came here just to tell you in person? I don't believe it. People don't travel two thousand miles to deliver news, even to a dear friend. That's what the postal service is for. If a letter won't do, the telegraph *has* made it all the way to Mountain Home."

He watched her closely, took note of her hesitancy to meet his gaze, the tightness of her mouth. She'd folded her arms in a defensive posture that screamed insecurity...and fear.

She *feared* August Rose. He'd put a stop to that. "He threatened you."

"No."

"He's sure as shootin' holding something over your head, and I won't stand for it."

"He *did not* threaten me." She actually looked at him then.

"If he didn't threaten you, why are you afraid?"

"Because he plans to stay in town." She shivered and briskly rubbed her upper arms to warm herself. She seemed so small, so defenseless.

Luke didn't like the idea of August Rose staying, but he needed to understand why Effie didn't like it. "This is a problem because...?"

"He thinks there's a possibility for us, for he and I..."

His gut clenched. "Why would he think that?"

"Years ago, before I married, Gus and I were too young to know better. We fell in love—it was brief, misguided, and over quickly." She waved a hand as if to dissipate the memory.

Ouch. He didn't like knowing she'd once loved Rose, but at least she didn't claim to fancy him now.

"Gus seems to believe there's hope for us to rekindle that youthful romance."

Luke weighed her answer against the level of anxiety he'd seen with his own two eyes...and it didn't reconcile. Effie had proved herself too level-headed, too rational, too reasonable a woman to tremble with barely suppressed emotion just because an old beau had reemerged and expressed interest.

No. There was more to it than what she'd disclosed.

He'd get to the bottom of it.

But first, he had railway tickets to return to their rightful owner. As much as he dreaded confronting an armed U.S. Marshal, he looked forward to making himself clear. It was time August Rose left town—*alone.*

Luke found August Rose in the boarding house dining room. From the slump of his shoulders and contemplative expression, the fella had a lot on his mind.

But not so much he'd let his guard down. He sat with his back to the wall, in full view of the front door.

At this hour, Mrs. Ihnken prepared breakfast. Aromas of cooking meat and frying potatoes wafted through the warm house. Footsteps sounded overhead in the second story bedrooms for let.

Luke was pleased to find he had August's attention to himself. No sense having this conversation with an audience.

August stood, and to Luke's surprise, offered a handshake.

He hesitated, just a beat. He wouldn't read too much into this. He closed the distance and accepting the gesture of greeting.

"Morning." Rose's grip was sure and strong, warm from the ceramic of his coffee cup and many long minutes near the fire in the dining room hearth.

"Morning."

"Come for breakfast? Mrs. Ihnken makes mighty fine steak and eggs."

"No. I came to see you."

August lifted a brow in question.

Luke tossed the tickets onto the table. "It's time you left town."

The other man heard, naturally, but didn't give much of a response. Luke hadn't expected this to be easy, but neither had he expected August to take it so calmly.

Slowly, August's storm-gray eyes hardened to granite. He took his chair with an insolence that made Luke's hackles rise. Seconds ticked past on Mrs. Ihnken's grandfather clock in the front parlor.

Luke ached to fill the silence with reasons, good and valid reasons why a gentleman would accept Effie's refusal and board today's train. He bit his tongue and waited. He knew a thing or two about tackling sticky subjects with men he didn't like...managing the ranch had given him too much practice.

Finally, Rose set down his coffee cup, the barely audible clatter against saucer emphasizing his fine self-control. Luke's estimation of the other man improved—though he didn't like it.

"Time, you say." August quirked one brow.

"Mrs. O'Leary has made her wishes known. Accept it and move on."

Something like a smile ghosted across his mouth. "O'Leary, huh?"

Luke had the sudden urge to throw Mrs. Ihnken's fine dining room chair across the table and clobber August Rose with it.

"I do believe," August said evenly, "I know a great deal more 'bout what my lady wants, as I've known Euphemia Scofield Carmichael since we were young."

Carmichael?

Luke's gut clenched. He fought to hide the visceral reaction, to tamp down the jumble of questions the loaded statement provoked. He thrashed every memory but came up empty. He'd never heard Effie use any other name—just O'Leary.

Obviously, August Rose knew that.

So she'd married an O'Leary since parting ways with Rose...who didn't know she had.

Maybe.

What, exactly, was the man saying?

"If you intend to slander Mrs. O'Leary's good name, persuade her to use that blasted train ticket you bought—"

"Hold your horses," August interrupted. "You imply I'd spread falsehoods about my future wife."

Luke's temper flashed white-hot—*future wife?* "She refused you."

"You couldn't be more wrong."

Luke's heart pounded at a fast gallop. Surely Effie had refused his proposal just like she'd refused to leave town.

All the clatter in the kitchen came to a sudden and evident halt. No doubt Mrs. Ihnken listened in, aware a tantalizing conversation transpired. She probably had an ear pressed to the door separating kitchen from dining room.

Luke chose his words with care, though he wanted to take August Rose outside and settle this with his fists. Luke's fury had gathered enough steam he figured he could have the lawman trussed like a calf inside thirty seconds.

He drew a steadying breath. "Not five minutes ago, I heard *her decision.* She stays." He pushed away from the ladder-back chair. "And you,

Marshal, will be on the afternoon train back to wherever you came from. *Alone.*"

"That so?"

"Accept defeat like a man and go."

"Can't do that. Effie might need a little persuading, but I believe she'll come around. I won't leave until she agrees to accompany me."

The taunt sliced close to home. Luke narrowed his gaze. "That's not going to happen. She doesn't love you, not anymore."

"Maybe," August said. "Maybe not. But she loved me deeply, not that long ago, and was eager to be my wife. It won't take much to rekindle that tender affection."

Effie glanced at her timepiece. Forty five minutes remained until she needed to open the shop. Just enough time to cut out the yellow flannel set Hunter Kendall had ordered for his wife. The task would hopefully calm the racing thoughts Luke's questions had caused.

He wanted to understand her behavior last night and this morning. He'd be back—soon, later, tomorrow, it didn't matter. He *would* return. And he'd expect answers.

She'd just unrolled the fabric on her cutting table and reached for the pattern pieces when a knock sounded on her shop's door.

Luke waved to her through the display window. Her shoulders sagged. She might as well get this over with.

She unlocked the door and ushered him inside. "You returned his tickets?"

He nodded as he removed his hat and unwound a thick, knitted scarf. His cheeks were pink from the wind. He pulled off his gloves and hung his coat on the peg on her back wall—as if he intended this conversation to take a while.

"I came to say what I should've said last Sunday or last October or anytime at all. I thought I had time. I thought *we* had time."

His subject caught her off guard—she'd been prepared to explain her behavior since Gus arrived, not *this*...

"I'd intended to wait for your mourning to draw to a close, for your widow's weeds to give way to gray or purple."

Her pulse quickened. "Luke—"

He took a step closer, gestured for silence. She caught the scent of winter wind on his clothes, a hint of horse and man mingled and was so uniquely him.

"Let me finish. I don't know how to put this in words, so I'm just going to say it. This past year and a half, every time I came for you for Sunday dinner at my parents' table, every time I escorted you to Founder's Day or took you on a drive, I was just biding my time, waiting to declare myself. I'm doing that now."

His protectiveness last night made infinitely more sense. He hadn't acted merely out of neighborly concern—he'd behaved like a beau. And somehow, she'd never suspected he'd taken interest in her. How had she not noticed?

He cupped her elbows, tugged ever so gently as if leading in a dance step, an invitation for an embrace. She hesitated—but how she wanted to. But allowing herself the comfort would convey entirely the wrong message.

Unmistakable honesty filled his hazel eyes. "You said you don't like the idea of August Rose staying in town, that you're not interested in marrying him. That's good, because you captured my interest the moment you moved to Mountain Home, and I've not considered another woman since. I intend to win your heart."

Emotion surged out of nowhere. She wanted to laugh—or maybe cry. She pressed four fingertips to her mouth to hide the trembling. She shook her head.

Why must two men challenge her resolve at the same time? True, Gus had been little temptation. But Luke's interest was an entirely different matter. For him, she wanted to reconsider, and that scared her.

"Give me a chance here, Effie. I'm not asking you to marry me...yet. I intend to win your heart, bit by bit, thread by thread, until I own the masterpiece. *Then* I'll ask you to be my wife."

Stand firm, she commanded herself. *The decision is made.*

"Now that you know my intentions, I feel I have a right to ask what's bothering you...and expect an answer." His touch swept up her arms to her shoulders. "When I showed up here last night, you were anxious, worried, not yourself. I saw your fear, and it was a whole lot more than nervousness over a long-ago beau, far more than tiredness at the end of a trying day. *Tell me.*"

Her heart pounded and her mouth turned dry as a July afternoon.

She straightened and eased back from his gentle touch. Gentle fondness lit his remarkable hazel eyes. She basked in that warmth, knowing it wouldn't last.

He wasn't one to gossip and she couldn't believe he'd hurt her by spreading a word of what she would share with him. He'd brought it up before leaving to return the train tickets to Gus. It wouldn't be easy, but at least she was prepared.

He must've seen the sadness sweeping over her, for he tipped her chin up with a gentle nudge of his knuckle. "You can tell me. I'll help. Nothing is so bad we can't get through it together."

His kindness overwhelmed her. She turned away, wishing with all her heart things were different.

She knew him through and through. In the year and a half of friendship with him and his family she'd come to know his nature and temperament. He had no secrets—he'd be appalled by hers.

"I'm not who you think I am. I've done terrible, unforgivable things."

She felt more than heard Luke draw close behind her. His hand settled on her shoulder. That quiet show of support and understanding poured into her as if she borrowed his strength. She felt no judgment from him—how was that possible?

"I married a man of my father's choosing at age seventeen. I never loved him, my husband, and his cruelty turned my distaste for him to pure hatred." Old memories surfaced, terrors she'd thought she'd put behind her. There'd been too much talk of Reuben Carmichael since Gus's arrival.

The dark stains on her soul seemed as visible as mud on the hem of a skirt. "I hated him."

Luke's warm hand circled slowly between her shoulder blades, comforting, soothing. He waited, silently, but his acceptance was too much. How could he listen to the ugliness within her, and *want* to touch her?

"He locked me in my room. Starved me for days on end. Cut off my communication with parents, sister, and friends." She'd never told a soul about the depravity within her marriage, and speaking of it now caused an odd disconnect...almost as if she spoke of someone else. "After one particularly difficult week, I struck him with a crystal vase. I'm not proud of it...I *wanted* to kill him."

In the eyes of the law, intent mattered more than outcome.

She held perfectly still, expecting him to halt, gather his things, and let himself out. He wasn't one to raise his voice at a woman, and certainly not his fists. But she knew he would not call on her again—there would be no courtship, and that was good...just what she wanted. He'd remove his little sister from her employ, and that would be that.

But he moved closer, until the warmth of his chest pressed against her back. His hands settled on her waist. The heat of his breath stirred the hairs at her left ear as he pressed a kiss to her temple.

Her heart leapt at the contact. His kiss communicated...forgiveness?

She crossed her arms and rested her hands upon Luke's. She craved his embrace and the absolution he foolishly offered. "Do you understand now?"

"Hmm?"

"I believed Gus had come to arrest me, to stand trial for murder—at least attempted murder."

He wrapped his arms about her middle, embracing her. "Seems that's not why he came to Colorado."

She found her head resting against his shoulder and cheek. She shouldn't give in to him like this...but it felt too wonderful, like the comfort of relaxing into bed after a long day on her feet, yet immeasurably better.

She shouldn't mislead him. She would pull away...after one more minute.

"Is this what you two talked about last night?" He snuggled her a little closer and encircled his arms about her waist.

"Yes. I believed he'd come to arrest me—I was wrong. He simply brought news. My parents passed away within a short while of one another.

And that my husband *did* die—but not by my hand as I'd assumed. He died last winter."

"I'm sorry about your parents." He paused. "About the husband...that's good."

Suddenly, Effie needed to see Luke's expression more than she needed his warmth and support. She turned, pulling free of his grasp easily, and searched his clear gaze.

Acceptance. Calm understanding. There *must* be more to it. It wasn't possible—even for kindhearted Luke—that he took the news this well.

She didn't deserve forgiveness. Or understanding.

"I lied to everyone in Mountain Home," she pressed. "I lied to you."

His dark brows pulled together. "Doesn't matter."

"Yes, it does. I passed myself off as a widow when in fact, I could've been a murderess—I *believed* myself to be a murderess. I was a runaway wife."

He shrugged. "If you'd had another way out, you'd have taken it."

"I lied about my name. I picked O'Leary from thin air. My name is Euphemia Eugenia Scofield Carmichael."

"I know."

What? Her jaw fell slack. "How? How do you know?"

"August told me. Just before I returned. I told him to leave town, and he retaliated with your full name, to substantiate his claim that he knows you better. He left out Eugenia."

She squeezed her eyes shut, disappointed at Gus's betrayal. How *could* he? Was he trying to discredit her so she'd leave with him?

"How are you not angry?" Reuben would've locked her in her room for three days, forbade the household help from unlocking the door for *any* reason.

He shrugged. "Should I be?"

"Yes. What man wouldn't be furious to find a woman lied to him?"

"Your husband might have been that kind of man, Effie, but I assure you, I'm not. My father isn't. Hunter isn't. Compassionate men exist."

"Not for me, they don't. This is why I will *never* subject myself to a man's control. I won't marry. You deserve to know this."

A smile tugged at one corner of his mouth. He brought his knuckles to her cheek, goose bumps rising in the wake of his feather-light touch. "Thanks for explaining yourself. It makes perfect sense that you avoid marriage because I'm *not* angry."

"That's not what I meant—"

He took his time lowering his head to kiss first one cheek and then the other.

"W-what are you doing?"

Despite the alarm clanging in her head, warning her to pull away, she desperately wanted to turn into his kiss, to seek his lips with her own. So very forward, so rash, but for the first time since she'd been young and foolish and hiding her budding romance with Gus, she found herself *wanting* a man's kiss.

This was dangerous—so very dangerous. It threatened her determination.

He eased back before she could act on the urge—probably best, given everything. He needed time to think things through. He'd come to his senses.

His callused thumb stroked the line of her jaw. "Just so there's no misunderstanding, Mrs. O'Leary, I heard you. I heard every word."

"Good. I'm glad you understand courtship isn't possible, that I will not marry again."

"I understand. I also intend to change your mind."

Anticipation tingled within her. She nearly groaned in frustration.

"All you need," he soothed, "is the right man...and I aim to prove *I am* that man."

"No. You're wasting your time. I'm firm in my resolve—"

"I won't push you into anything. But given everything you said, it's only fair you know I'm firm in *my* resolve, Effie O'Leary—I aim to win your heart."

"I can't. I don't have time." Effie shifted the cotton flannel on her cutting block, set the pinking iron, and whacked it harder than necessary. "I have too much work to conscience taking the evening off."

Gus's lopsided smile had once won her over completely. Now it just irritated her, so she kept her focus on her task. She zipped through another six inches before he spoke.

"You've got to eat sometime."

"I will eat." *Whack.* "I'll stop for a bite once I'm done with this process."

He grabbed the mallet from her hand.

She squawked in protest. "Give that back."

Nudging her out of the way, he set to work pinking the cut edge with astonishing accuracy. She couldn't fault his skill.

He glanced at her. "I'm a man of many skills."

She snagged Mayor Abbott's suit coat from the stool and found needle and thread. She'd keep busy, dig into another waiting project. If she couldn't persuade Gus to believe she didn't have time to dine out with him tonight with words, then she'd show him with action.

She sat at her machine where the light was best and threaded a sewing needle. She whipped a basting stitch into the cap of the sleeve and watched Gus turn the nightgown's front panel around and continued pinking the cut edge.

"I think a hot meal would do you good. I worry you're not eating right."

She glared at him.

He chuckled. "All you eat is bread and cold meat. What about vegetables? Potatoes and gravy?"

"If you haven't noticed," she told him,

offering what she hoped was a stern expression, "I don't live a life of ease, Mr. Rose. I haven't a kitchen of my own nor time to cook so I eat simply."

The rhythmic pounding of the mallet against pinking iron fell into an easy cadence. "Aren't you hungry for good food?"

"No." She decided to change the subject. "Where did you learn to pink that well?"

"Necessity, dear Effie. Necessity."

"Did you work as a tailor's assistant?"

He chuckled, dropping the finished panel onto the cutting table and picking up its companion. "Nope."

"You're not going to tell me anything, are you?"

"I will, over dinner. Put on your cloak. I'm starving."

She thrust the needle in and out of the seam allowance in a precise running stitch. "Don't let me keep you."

"You're grumpy."

She glared at him, again.

He grinned, as if blind to her frustration. "You know, if you'd take an hour here and there for yourself, rest a bit throughout your work day, you wouldn't be so stressed."

"I don't have the luxury of taking an hour off, not at this time of year. If I want to sleep seven or eight hours tonight, I have to put in a full day's work."

"If I help you, you'll have time to break for

dinner. Look, I'm already done with all these edges. Not a one will fray. Even and beautiful, too." He swept the yellow scraps into a cupped hand and dropped them into the waste basket.

"Thank you." Gus was right, she was a grump.

"Come to dinner with me." He offered her his hand, his tone softer and more of a question than a command. Perhaps the man could be taught.

She lowered the suit sleeve to her lap. She gestured helplessly at the stack of garments in various stages of completion.

"We'll eat, and I promise we won't linger. When your stomach's full and you're feeling less irritable," he winked at her, his happy disposition shining through, "we'll come right back here and get to work. I'm mighty good at pinning things together—could hand them off to you ready to sew."

Her stomach rumbled and the mere thought of a sit-down dinner with hot food nearly had her giving in.

"How 'bout it?"

She knew what was behind his dinner invitation—what was behind his presence in the shop this late afternoon. And she couldn't allow him to misconstrue anything. She had to ensure he understood. "You do realize sharing a meal doesn't mean anything has changed. We're friends...and that's all we can ever be."

"I'll get your cloak."

On Thursday, Luke delegated every responsibility on the ranch and informed the crew and his family he'd spend the day in town with Effie.

Five long days had dragged by since she'd confided her past and he'd told her it didn't make him think less of her. He intended to court her, win her heart, and wed her. Nothing had changed. But if he didn't get into town and act like it, Effie would doubt his sincerity...and August Rose would have the greater advantage.

He hadn't stayed away intentionally, and wasn't a man to play games. But his dedication to the ranch and his family had interrupted his courting plans—everything from a heavy snowfall to illness among the hired hands that left them four men down.

First thing, he'd bathed, shaved, put on his best clothes, selected a book from the shelf in the parlor, and hitched up the sleigh to take Noelle in to work.

He decided to greet Effie before he took care of the horse and sleigh. He grinned broadly as he ushered his sister through Pettingill's front door.

The door was unlocked, though the shop wasn't officially open and no customers were inside.

"Good morning, Noelle." Effie sounded good. Like herself. It was so good to see the anxiety and fear of last week gone.

"Morning, Miss Noelle. Luke." *August.* There

he was, behind the counter, sitting on a stool...sewing buttons on a crisp white shirt?

Gus grinned. Widely. He looked absurd, a rough-and-tough lawman *sewing*. He swept the needle through the eye on the back of the button and as if he'd done the chore a thousand times before.

He sewed with the same ease Luke's sisters, mother, and Effie displayed.

For some reason, Luke detested the idea that Gus possessed a skill Effie appreciated.

He should've known the competition would already be here, though he'd had Effie to himself for five days. He felt like booting Gus into the street and claiming the next five days for himself.

Noelle hung up her coat and immediately set to work.

Luke noticed August's gaze followed Noelle to the cutting table where she picked up scissors.

Luke used the distraction to approach Effie. Her dimpled smile was all the encouragement he needed. He clasped her elbow and pressed a kiss to her forehead. "I missed you."

"It's a surprise to see you here." Gus said.

Luke ignored the interloper. The man knew exactly why Luke was here. They'd made themselves clear last they met.

"I'm glad to see you." Effie's dimples deepened.

His heart kicked. When she looked at him like that he felt ten feet tall.

"What brings you in?" she asked, but the light

dancing in her eyes made it evident she already knew.

He couldn't help but grin. Why had he waited so long to declare himself? He liked the awareness in her eyes.

"I'm here to spend the day with you."

"Good thing," Gus interrupted. "Effie has three packages ready for delivery. Don't unhitch your sleigh just yet."

Luke glared at Gus, but the agitator's attention was on his sewing and missed it.

"Oh, would you?" Effie spared Luke another smile and collected the precisely wrapped bundles from the counter. "That would help me ever so much. I'd thought I'd have to hire a Murphy boy to deliver them for me *if* he could get away from the store."

Now Gus looked up and smirked.

How long had it taken August Rose, U.S. Marshal to come up with this plan to get Luke out of the way for a few hours?

Luke's jaw ached from clenching his jaw. He intentionally relaxed and determined to play this to his advantage. "For you, Effie, I'm glad to." He slipped an arm about her middle and gave her a little squeeze.

"Wonderful."

"Where to?" He searched the crisp paper wrapping for Effie's pencil script with the owner's name and her notation of amount due, if any, locating it just as she touched a finger to one corner.

"I'd go, but don't have any idea where these customers live." Gus knotted off his thread and snipped it with miniature embroidery scissors.

Luke had to admit the other man displayed a flair for finish work, and it was obvious by the lengthy list of projects detailed in Effie's ledger, open on the counter, she needed the help.

Gus pulled a new length of white thread off a spool and threaded the needle with deft hands. "I'm of more help here."

Must he point that out? Luke might know where everyone lived, but Gus had the upper hand...he was useful *in* the shop.

Gus's smile turned smug. "We'll have another two or three packages ready to go by the he gets back, won't we, Sweetheart?"

Luke's guts clenched and he had the sudden urge to attack. *Sweetheart?*

Effie didn't seem to notice the term of endearment *or* Gus's meddling.

There wasn't enough room in this shop for two suitors.

One way or the other, he had to find a way to spend time with her, alone. On top of that, he still had to come up with viable ways to win her heart, one thread at a time.

Unfortunately, had absolutely no idea how to make that happen.

Five

By dusk, Luke had delivered nine packages, all around the valley. Each time he stopped back at the shop to give Effie the money he'd collected and report on the successful deliveries, Gus had presented him with one or more bundles.

If Effie hadn't been so delighted with the help, he would've quit long ago.

But the time he spent out in the cold had proved effective, because now he had a plan he felt good about implementing.

He knocked on the Sheriff's office door and let himself in. The space felt gloriously warm and the scent of strong coffee welcoming.

Liam Talmadge glanced up from the newspaper on his desk. "Well, I'll be. I hear you're working as Mrs. O'Leary's delivery boy."

If Liam weren't as old as dirt, Luke might take offense. "That's actually why I'm here. I need your help."

All traces of jesting melted from the sheriff's lined face. "You see somethin' while you were out?"

"No. Things are peaceful."

Liam relaxed. "Coffee?"

"Sounds good. I'm froze clear through."

Once cups were poured and Liam reclaimed his seat, he asked, "What kind of help do you need?"

"You've met the stranger in town, I suppose."

"The U.S. Marshal. O'course."

"He's not here in official capacity. His name's August Rose."

Talmadge nodded, apparently conceding the point.

"He's also making a nuisance of himself. Underfoot constantly, won't give Mrs. O'Leary five minutes to herself. He's attracting so many curious folk, her shop's crowded and she's got plenty to do as it is."

Liam sipped, holding Luke's gaze over the rim of his cup.

"Looks to me like the problem's a simple one."

"I want your help with a simple solution—we've got to put August to work. Somewhere besides Mrs. O'Leary's shop."

"You're sweet on her. That's the simple problem."

Luke had no trouble admitting it. "I am. I'm

courting her, just spoke to her about it last weekend."

Talmadge's smile twinkled with a bit too much enjoyment. "Mr. August Rose, it seems, believes he's courting her, too."

"She refused him. Won't even consider him, thank God." The old man's gaze had Luke fidgeting. "It makes sense you deputize him or something."

"You lookin' for a fighting chance with her, son?"

That question didn't need an answer. The sheriff knew Luke couldn't court his gal with the interloper constantly underfoot.

Talmadge nodded. "I got an idea or two."

"I've got plenty of suggestions: snow removal, street patrol, cover your hours here. Tell him you're sick and need the next three weeks off."

He chuckled. "When do you want him to start?"

"Right now."

"Do you have another lamp?" Luke set aside the book he'd read aloud for the past hour. "You need more light and so do I."

The fine tale—*A Cricket on the Hearth*—had helped pass the time. She'd enjoyed it more for the resonance, cadence, and rhythm of Luke's voice. The quality of his reading caught her by surprise. After all, he was a rancher, not a schoolteacher, not a writer like Dickens himself, not an actor upon a stage.

"One. On the table in the back room." She turned the balance wheel, sank the needle, and lifted the presser foot to exact a crisp turn at the collar's point.

Luke soon had the lamp filled and wick lit. He lifted it high. "How is this?"

"Better, but you can't stand there holding it indefinitely."

Luke set the lamp on the counter. "You can't work in such meager light." He shrugged into his coat and pulled on his gloves. "I've an idea. Give me five minutes."

He returned quickly. Snow, ice, and bitter wind swirled inside with him, though he'd had the door open mere seconds. Another gust rattled the window panes. A damp chill cut through her heavy winter petticoats and lined wool suit.

Luke plunked a small paper-wrapped bundle onto the counter top and shed his coat. "Brackets to hold your lamps on the wall."

"Brackets?" Why hadn't she thought of that?

"Yes. I can't have you losing your eyesight when it's preventable."

He noticed her needs, acted in kindness, attended to her comfort. How could she not adore him? "I can see."

"I'll go blind if I have to read another page in the dark."

She chuckled. "I didn't ask you to stay." She knew he wouldn't go, not until she retired for the night. He'd been a constant fixture for the past two days, since he'd worked hard all day making her deliveries.

She'd heard talk of Gus working with Sheriff Talmadge, but didn't know what to think of it.

"You didn't need to ask. I'm here 'cause I want to be."

He measured each side of the window, from floor on up, and marked a spot with pencil. He'd chosen well. The lamps would be out of the way and yet shed maximum light on her work.

"It's far too cold to head home tonight. Domino is bedded down in the livery, and I'll take a room at the boarding house. I'll head home once the sun is up. Can't risk Domino on a night like this."

"No, I imagine you can't." She smiled and shook her head at his transparent efforts to stay with her until bedtime. His attention felt good, flattering, and she enjoyed his company. If it weren't for the expectation of marriage, she rather liked courtship.

It was all so new...and surprisingly enjoyable. Reuben Carmichael had not courted her for there'd been no need. Just an agreement between him and her father and it was done.

She kept the sewing machine whirring and completed the collar's facing. Her back ached from sitting so long in one place, so she moved to stand at the ironing board to run a basting stitch through the cap of the sleeves.

With her chair vacated, he leaned across her

sewing machine cabinet and finished affixing the burning lamps to the wall, tightening the brackets with care.

She watched him work in the flickering light. He flashed her a happy grin as he picked up the second lamp and turned to the bracket on the other side of the window.

By the time she'd eased one sleeve into the armhole and secured the seam with pins, Luke had completed his task.

"Come see if the light is better."

She smiled as he tucked the chair beneath her. Aware of his nearness, she tucked the seam under the presser foot and spun the balance wheel to start the machine. Rocking the treadle, she continued around the armhole, removing pins as she went. "The improvement is significant." She met his gaze in the reflection of the window. "*Thank* you."

His hands settled on her shoulders. Their reflection against the dark night beyond was almost as crisp as a mirror, enhanced by newly positioned lamplight.

This picture of him standing behind her chair, his hands upon her shoulders, affected her more than she wanted to admit. This was a glimpse of the path their lives could take...*if* she dared. He'd suggested, a week ago, this conjoined future. Despite her refusal to take out the forbidden idea and turn it over in her mind, his declaration had ignited a yearning within her.

Could she?

She met his gaze and couldn't miss the longing there.

Time seemed to slow, elongate, in the dreamlike way some poignant moments do.

She wanted—no, *needed*—to look away, for she feared she wore a similar expression. He'd notice, and it would be ever so much harder to keep him at a distance.

At last he lowered his gaze. She watched, transfixed, unwilling to move as his fingers caught an errant wisp of her hair and rubbed it between his fingers. He focused wholly on her. Undeniable affection shone in his countenance.

His sincerity caused a subtle shift within her—and evoked a desire to open her heart.

This realization should have induced frustration if not outright disappointment...but it did not. She wanted the tingly sensation of his gentle tug on her hair and the comforting weight of his hand upon her shoulder. She wanted to watch him to her heart's content in the window's reflection. She simply...*wanted*.

In one week's time, in his absence and in his attentiveness, Luke Finlay had done the unthinkable...he'd shown her the better part she hadn't known existed. He'd made her *want*.

And just like that, her firm resolve and immovable determination lost its foundation of stone. She shuddered, a house built upon a foundation of sand.

"I'll carry in firewood. You'll need more before dawn."

He must've mistaken her shudder for a shiver. He released her hair and squeezed both shoulders in capable hands. "Tomorrow, Effie, I'm coming to get you for Sunday dinner."

She blinked, refocused her thoughts. She'd been lost in a sea of fanciful imaginings. *Sunday dinner*...another thing she found she genuinely wanted. "Thank you, but I can't. I have two short weeks 'til Christmas."

"All the more reason why you need a day off. You need a break from these four walls. You need a rest. You need to relax. You *need* family."

He was right, of course. She needed as well as wanted.

Was it possible to guard her heart against this man?

On Monday morning Effie held the door open while Luke carried in the small stove he intended to install in her back room. On the way back to town last night after Sunday dinner with the Finlays, Luke had told her of his intentions to give her this second stove. His motives were pure—he simply wanted to see her adequately warm.

It was his idea, a Christmas gift, he'd insisted, and he would do the work himself.

Noelle waved in her good-natured manner as she followed Luke inside. She hung up her coat and set immediately to work.

Everyone in the valley trusted the Finlays.

They all followed through and did exactly what they'd committed to. As Effie heard Luke unpacking the crate in her private quarters, she figured that strength was also her greatest danger.

Luke had vowed to win her heart, bit by bit, and that's exactly what he'd done. He had her doubting her resolutions, wondering if she had the capacity for love.

She'd simply have to ignore him, concentrate on her customers and her work, and keep him at a distance.

As she'd lain in bed this morning, dreading another day with Luke near, she'd rehearsed a lengthy list of reasons why she was better off unmarried, why she was far happier alone. She squared her shoulders. She could do this. She *would* do this.

Mrs. Abbott, the mayor's wife, came in shortly after nine to collect her orders. As Effie showed each item to Mrs. Abbott for her inspection, she couldn't help but hear every rasp of the saw, every clank of iron stovepipe against wood. She was far too attuned to Luke. As they'd agreed, the door remained open. Customer curiosity would peak if they couldn't see for themselves.

Unfortunately, this meant Effie could watch Luke at work. With his shirtsleeves rolled up and sawdust clinging to his jeans, he looked more a carpenter than a rancher.

Effie pulled her gaze away. She didn't want to see the play of muscles beneath his shirt nor acknowledge the breadth of his shoulders.

"I see the rumors can't be true," Mrs. Abbott said, leaning over the counter as if to confide secrets. "If young Mr. Finlay's going to all that work installing another stove on your premises, you can't be leaving town."

Effie looked up from folding Mrs. Abbott's gabardine skirt. "Who said I was leaving?"

"Why, that handsome U.S. Marshal of yours did. But I see you're simply adding value to the operation so it fetches a better price." Mrs. Abbott softened her words with a wink. "Mighty fine business sense you have, Mrs. O'Leary."

"Effie's not going anywhere." Noelle tore off a length of brown paper. "She's told Mr. Rose so. I think he doesn't want to believe her."

The last thing Effie wanted was to add to the gossip mill, so she took the matching blouse Mrs. Abbott held and exchanged it with the shirt she'd just finished for the mayor. "Is the blouse to your liking? Good. Please take a look at the mayor's new shirt."

Ann Abbott had to be the most particular of Effie's customers. Once Effie had proved her skills met Mrs. Abbott's expectations, the inspection before payment had become a mere formality.

"Most handsome." Ann admired the plackets at the sleeve's cuff, fingered a buttonhole or two, and smoothed the expensive cotton with a palm. "You do excellent work."

"Thank you, Mrs. Abbott." Effie knew what would come next. As far as Mrs. Abbott was concerned, her orders, no matter when placed, should take precedence over any others. Her husband was the mayor, after all.

"How is your work on the mayor's new suit progressing?"

Right on cue. Effie couldn't help but smile.

Noelle, quick to please, brought out the suit coat. "Have you ever touched wool this soft and fine?"

As Noelle kept Mrs. Abbott occupied, Effie opened the ledger to make notations of the garments Mrs. Abbott had collected and tally the bill. Payment was accepted, pleasantries exchanged, and it wasn't long and Mrs. Abbott left, her arms full and a smile on her face.

Effie put an arm about Noelle's shoulders. "You're a gem."

"You're the one who knows just what to say to her. She scares me."

Effie chuckled. She'd once had all of Hartford's Society at her feet. She could handle the upper crust of Mountain Home. "She's not so bad. She simply wants to feel important and respected."

Didn't everyone want the same?

She did.

And Luke had an uncanny way of ensuring she felt both—important and respected.

How was she supposed to resist softening even more to his charms?

Her traitorous heart was so attuned to Luke and his progress that it had started pounding with happy anticipation as she heard him finishing up. She forced herself to complete the seam before turning to him. He leaned in the doorway to her private room, his shirtsleeves still rolled up over forearms. Thick veins and dark hair enhanced the pull...so masculine and so familiar all at the same time.

"Want to see?" he asked.

Effie stood, noted Noelle had nearly finished the buttonholes on the mayor's suit coat. She took a moment to admire the perfect, tight stitching. "Very well done, Noelle. I do believe I owe you a raise. Your skills have improved, and you've earned it."

The girl's eyes lit with the same flair of happiness she often glimpsed in Luke's. The siblings—including Miranda—all had that same spark.

They ought to figure out how to bottle it. They'd make a fortune selling the patent medicine.

"You mean it?" Noelle's grin provoked a smile from Effie, too.

"Indeed I do. Next payday, a nice raise for you."

"Yes, ma'am—umm, Effie."

"When you're done there, you'll start sewing on the buttons?" She found the envelope containing the special-order leather-covered shank buttons Mrs. Abbott had insisted upon.

"Yes. Go see your stove."

Effie had a hard time meeting Luke's gaze. These two could see right through her, and no doubt recognized her attempt to delay joining Luke.

How pathetic was she?

It should be a simple thing, to admire his craftsmanship, thank him for a job well done, and offer—though he'd refuse—repayment for the hardware and compensation for his time.

What was *wrong* with her?

Butterflies flitted about her stomach and she couldn't help but smile...sure signs her recent flirtation with certain disaster wasn't entirely in the past.

Number one: I will not forfeit my hard-won freedom.

Number two: I am content with my life the way it is.

She would mentally recite her list as often and as frequently as required until the temporary infatuation passed. It *would* pass...she'd make sure of it.

Number three: Men are never the same after marriage as they appear beforehand.

Luke offered his hand. His expression conveyed such hope, such optimism she'd accept.

Effie split a glance between him and his little sister, and finding Noelle busily stitching by light from the window, she still hesitated.

Should she?

Was it really so bad, just to take his hand?

He simply waited, a soft smile playing about his lips. Oh! He *knew* how much conflict this caused her, and yet he offered his hand anyway.

Shame on him. She strode past him and into the bedroom, leaving him to follow.

She made sure she left him plenty of room so he didn't need to stand too near. With her attention entirely on the new appliance, she scanned it from ceiling to floor, noting he'd built a square base of bricks to keep the iron legs off the floorboards.

Luke had cleaned up every stray bit of sawdust. The stovepipe climbed straight and true, and, as she'd overheard from her sewing machine, he'd built a fire in the stove's belly.

He held out his hands to warm them. "Come try it out."

"I feel the warmth from here. Thank you, Mr. Finlay."

He quirked a brow. He seemed on the brink of laughter, but instead he snagged her wrist and pulled her forward. "I don't bite. What's the matter?"

She swallowed. "Not a thing."

Number four: Marriage is most disagreeable.

She determined to compliment him and get the conversation back on track. "You're a tidy worker."

"Tidy?" Now he did laugh. "Loosen up, Effie. You're talking to me like we're barely acquaintances."

He looped his arm about her shoulders, pulled her close. "And I think we're more than that. We're at least friends." He whispered the last of it close to her ear.

Predictably, her stomach tingled and her

body fairly sang at his touch. She fought to keep a straight face. "Yes, Mr. Finlay. We are friends."

"Is that all we are?" He nudged the shell of her ear with his nose, then his lips.

The delicious friction had her pulling away. "You know it's all we can be."

Number five: My nature is unsuited to marriage.

He shifted, cupped her face in his big hands, and his mouth touched hers for the briefest of seconds. He searched her gaze and asked a silent question.

Number six: I do not want male attention.

His hands trembled.

Sudden awareness flooded her system. All she could see, feel, *sense* was Luke. Warm, near, and focused wholly on her.

I'm a liar. I want this *man's attention.*

Intoxicating.

Exhilarating.

Her breath caught.

He looked her in the eye with an unguarded intensity she'd never experienced, never understood could happen between a man and a woman. He took her in, searching her gaze as if she were the most desirable woman in the world.

"Effie," he mouthed, silently, and kissed her.

His lips, so warm, so soft, sent an electrifying sensation bolting from lip to crown to toes. Her hands, flat against the flannel of his shirt, ached to steal into the hair at his nape.

His kiss stunned her in its simplicity and

utter reverence.

Never in her life—not even when she and Gus been young—had she experienced this kind of kiss.

Pure, wholesome, honest.

She understood demanding, rough kisses meant to subjugate and control.

She understood kisses devoid of tenderness.

She understood ungainly, forbidden kisses in carriage houses and moonlit gardens.

But *this*...

Her soul seemed to expand, bringing a sensation of exquisite joy quickly followed by panic...she could not allow herself to change her mind so easily.

Number six...no! Number seven: Men are undesirable.

That one—number seven—was a bald lie, it held no weight, and could not sustain her through moments of weakness.

This was most certainly one of those moments of excruciating weakness.

Luke Finlay *was* desirable.

So much more desirable for the innocence of his kiss.

He pulled back before she'd had a chance to savor—his kiss had been far too brief. In his eyes she glimpsed the most terrifying, awe-inspiring, *the* list-obliterating reason why this insanity must end.

Luke Finlay *loved* her.

Full, whole-hearted, bone-deep, life-long love. The same wordless communication she'd spied between Phil and Caroline, Luke's parents. A mirror image of the expression she'd seen in Hunter's eyes for Miranda.

Now, she understood.

Not once in her life—not even with Gus—had she experienced that utter, helpless, all-consuming love of a man, *for her*.

Her heart pounded with the realization she teetered on the verge of falling in love...*maybe*. Was she capable of the emotion?

A rush of hot tears threatened. It was simply too much.

She couldn't bear to let him see how he affected her, so she dipped her chin and alighted against him. She fit perfectly in the hollow of his throat.

His arms came about her, as if it were the most natural response. Beneath her hand, his heart thudded, quick and sure and strong.

The magnitude of her response to his kiss and the undeniable truth that he loved her changed everything. If his kiss hadn't moved her, if she'd not witnessed the depth of his affection, she might be able to set it aside with the ease in which she'd set Gus's kisses aside.

The two were simply incomparable.

An hour ago, she never would've believed she might so much as consider forfeiting her freedom and independence. Now, her whole world had shifted.

The shop door opened, tinkling bells carrying in the quiet.

Scissors thudded on the cutting table. Noelle's stool scraped against the floor. "Afternoon, Mr. Rose."

As Effie stiffened in his arms, Luke realized that how he played this trick hand he'd been dealt could change everything.

They'd come to a fork in the road. He wouldn't dare guess how far or how long, but for the moment, she'd chosen him. He didn't want to mess this up.

"Where's Effie off to?" Gus's boots thudded. Luke pictured Gus leaning a hip against the counter.

"She went out," Noelle said, "on errands."

The little minx. Fibbing to make sure Gus left, giving him more time alone with Effie. At least he knew which side his sister was on.

And he kind of liked it that Effie remained quiet, snuggled up against him, rather than go out to meet Gus.

He pressed his lips to her temple. She fit so perfectly in his arms, it seemed she'd always belonged there.

"Any idea when she'll be back?" Gus's voice carried easily through the open door.

"She didn't say. A good while, I suppose."

"Well, look at that." Gus's footfalls drew nearer, in the direction of the doorway into the bedroom. Well, if Gus walked in on them, saw Effie in Luke's arms, the decision would be taken from her and he knew, instinctively, she wouldn't like that.

He eased back enough to let her know this was up to her. If she wanted to stay right where she was, well, fine by him. But if this wasn't what she wanted Gus to see, she'd best step away.

He met her gaze and couldn't help but grin. The indecision on her pretty face was the most uncertain he'd ever seen her.

After she'd kissed him, really, was there anything left to work out? Beyond letting Gus know the matter was settled, Luke couldn't see anything else left to decide.

He felt like crowing.

Effie scowled at him and he felt the grin slide right off his face.

Oops.

Where Luke stood, he had a pretty good view of the doorway, but couldn't see Gus. Yet. Effie's back was turned more to the door than not. Of course she'd heard Gus, but hadn't a chance of seeing him unless she turned around.

She raised one shapely brow as if asking him a question.

"What?" he mouthed, careful not to make a sound. He couldn't read her expression.

With deliberate slowness, she leaned close and looped her arms about his middle. She had a smile on her face the size of Colorado as she dipped her chin and snuggled against his chest.

He realized what she intended—to show Gus how things were. And given he'd thought the same thing, himself, he really shouldn't be put out...but he was.

She'd decided to use him. Willful, intentional, plant-a-sign-in-the-snow to tell Gus a thing or two.

Gus's footfalls paused in the doorway.

Luke glanced up and met the other man's gaze. *Well, I'll be pickled.* Gus had a grin on his face. Luke would've expected a lot of things coming from a U.S. Marshal who'd just heard a tall tale from a shop clerk...who happened to be the competition's little sister.

Had Luke been in Gus's boots, he'd have been angry to see Effie in Gus's arms, hiding in the back room and avoiding saying hello.

But Gus and Luke were apparently two very different kinds, 'cause Gus kept up the show for both ladies.

Gus tipped his head toward the new stove. "Well, would you look at that."

Effie stiffened.

Ah, so that was Gus's game. Getting back at

Effie. For some reason, it felt like Gus was getting back at him, too.

Gus grinned. "Can't say I'm surprised."

"It's new," Noelle said from the shop, just loud enough for Luke to make out. "Just happened today."

"Good." Gus winked.

Winked! Uh-oh. The other guy had a plan cooking...that much was certain.

"It's far colder at this elevation, and I've about froze, myself, a couple nights this week. It's good Mrs. O'Leary's got herself a new stove. Had it put in this morning, did she?"

"Yes. Should I tell her you came by?" Noelle's voice retreated past the counter, into the customer half of the store.

Effie snuggled deeper against Luke's neck and he let himself enjoy it. Whatever Gus was playing at, he wouldn't let it ruin the enjoyment of finally having her in his arms. He smoothed a hand up her back. He savored it doubly, knowing it had to rankle Gus.

"Nah." A bit of joviality sparkled in Gus's tone as he met Luke's gaze directly. "No need. She knows I came by. And tell Luke this war isn't over, not by a long shot." Gus fell back from the doorway and his footfalls retreated to the front door.

Well, son of a gun. This should be interesting, seeing what scrimmage Gus would wage next. It seemed kind of pointless, given Effie had made her choice. That kiss still hummed in his brain like too much liquor...and he just couldn't see Effie kissing him like that and giving Gus more than the time of day afterward.

"Afternoon, Miss Finlay." Gus let himself out, setting the bells to jingling.

Effie pushed away, her cheeks flushed and her eyes bright. "*You.*"

"Me?" The woman didn't make a lick of sense.

"Did you *see* him in the doorway?" Her eyes narrowed with accusation.

Was there a correct response?

Apparently she didn't want an answer because she turned away, her skirts swirling.

"Oh, no you don't." He reached for her, caught her elbow. "Settle down and tell me what's wrong."

"If you don't know, I don't feel the need to enlighten you."

She tugged her arm free and he let her go. She stomped into the shop and Luke followed. Shameless, he was. He'd follow her anywhere.

"Did he see?" Effie questioned Noelle. "He saw, didn't he?"

"Hey, now," Luke jumped to his sister's defense, tried to calm Effie with the same low voice and slow movements he used when approaching a riled stallion. Or a mean bull. He couldn't help it...the comparison of his sweet Effie and a snorting bull was just too accurate at the moment...and a smile shoved his control aside.

"You think this is funny?" She whirled on him.

"Yes, ma'am, I do. You heard him. You knew

he was there, and you willingly and intentionally stepped into my arms. I saw the look in your eye, Effie O'Leary. You chose me."

"I did *not*."

Luke glanced at his sister for support. Noelle ducked her head and whipped a stitch with her needle. So much for help from his sister—he changed his mind. She didn't deserve a thanks after all.

"Mind telling me what this is all about, then?"

She growled in frustration, more agitated than he'd ever seen her.

He'd never felt more helpless. He'd seen females' moods swing fast like this, from all placid and happy to spitting mad inside a second and a half, but this was ridiculous. As far as he could see, he only did what she'd wanted him to do. "*You* hugged *me*."

"Only to make him see I meant every word I've said."

Ouch. That stung. But he'd known, at the time, she'd used him and she wasn't herself at the moment, so he let it slide. "What did you say? To him?"

"That I will remain a widow the rest of my life. I have no intention of remarrying, and he'd best let go of his grand plans to marry me here—or Connecticut—because I won't."

"Well, that's good news."

She glared at him.

He sobered right fast.

"What you seem to have missed," she said in a

tone of false calm, "is that this effects you, too. I will remain a widow the rest of my life."

"Of course you're a widow. Your husband died."

She made an inarticulate sound of frustration. He'd evidently said the wrong thing.

She drew a deep breath and blew it out. She clasped her hands at her waist and just like that, she'd regained her composure—sort of. "Let me make myself clear. I refused Gus, and I refuse your courtship, too. I'm never getting married—"

"You kissed me like it meant something." He took a step closer.

He must've looked and sounded far more menacing than he'd intended 'cause Noelle shrieked and hopped down from the stool. "I'm headed to the necessary." She grabbed her coat and fled out the back door.

He'd bet a quarter dollar his sister had no interest in the outhouse. She'd simply seen and heard enough.

Luke focused his gaze on Effie. She shrank back, the wind gone from her sails.

Without another soul in the shop, he had no reason not to end this ridiculous argument once and for all. He reached for this woman, this beautiful, usually sweet and kind, normally gracious and good-hearted woman.

He loved her. He couldn't help it. Something had awoken inside him the first time he'd seen her, on the boardwalk in front of this very shop, that summer day a year and a half ago. And that something had reared on its hind legs not five minutes ago when he'd kissed her and she'd kissed him back. He may not have a wealth of experience with women, but he knew *this* woman. *His* woman.

She was confused. Angry at herself, upset at the loss of control with the situation. She'd wanted to show Gus a thing or two, and instead, Gus had turned the tables on her and shown her far more. Her pride smarted. She didn't know what to do about him, either, Luke figured. That kiss had changed things for her, too. He knew it just like he knew Noelle wouldn't be back anytime soon.

As if it were the most natural thing in the world, as if he'd held her every day of their lives, Luke put his arms around her and tugged her close. She stiffened, fighting him half-heartedly for only a second or two.

She seemed to melt like spring snow on a warm afternoon. She sagged and leaned on him, clutching the back of his shirt in her fists. "I'm sorry."

"It's okay, Effie. Take your time."

Two days later, Effie returned from making a deposit at the bank to find Gus and Luke squaring off across her sales counter. They both had elbows propped on the oak surface and flexed their hands in preparation for an arm wrestle.

At the sound of the door, Luke glanced over his shoulder. He'd braced his feet wide, providing an impressive view of muscled legs, taut backside, and broad shoulders. "There you are. You're just in time."

She propped hands upon her hips. "In time for what?"

"We're settling this, once and for all." All traces of Gus's usual joviality had disappeared.

"Settling what, exactly?" She didn't like the sound of this. But at least they hadn't determined to settle their differences with pistols—*yet*.

Neither man looked her way. They glared at one another, poised to grip hands like rams set to butt heads.

"Answer me."

"I told this drifter *I will* accompany you to the Annual Children's Program—"

Incensed, she cut Luke off. "*Drifter?*"

Gus chuckled. "I believe he called me an interloper, first go 'round."

She stalked closer, ready to knock their heads together. "This is my place of business. You can't *arm wrestle* to determine who might *ask* me to that event."

Luke grasped Gus's hand, flexing his fingers for a better hold. The men stared one another down, their heads lowered to maximize leverage.

This was entirely ridiculous. "Just so you know, I *do* have a say in the matter, and my answer is no. I won't go with either of you. So there's no sense going through with this."

Gus flexed, pulling hard, but Luke held steady. Muscles bulged beneath shirtsleeves. Strain showed on both faces.

Gus gained several inches, forcing Luke's backward. Their arms shook with strain.

She groaned in frustration, refusing to watch this ridiculous show. She hung up her cloak. "Where did you scare Noelle off to this time?"

They ignored her. Her temper spiked.

One man—perhaps both—grunted.

She couldn't help but notice Luke had regained the upper hand. He had Gus on the defense now. Perspiration beaded on his forehead and dampened his hair.

Let them battle this out, but if they thought she'd cooperate as the prize, they'd find themselves sorely disappointed.

She yawned, dramatically, making plenty of noise and patting her open mouth with exaggerated motions.

Neither so much as glanced her way as they remained locked in their contest.

The door opened. Of course it did, middle of the day like this. She'd hoped to find Noelle returning, but her luck wasn't that good. She decided to meet her patrons in the entryway. "Mrs. Cheney, Mrs. Talmadge, good afternoon to you both."

The matrons split down the middle and leaned around Effie for a better view.

"Are they...arm wrestling?" Doc Cheney's wife seemed captivated by the vision of Luke's strong back. Sweat had dampened his shirt and made the fabric cling to his skin.

"Whatever for?" Mrs. Talmadge, never one to wait idly by, strode directly for the counter to better see the main attraction.

"They're trying to prove a point." So far, all they'd proved was their adolescent need to best one another—and the striking similarity in their strength. Their arms shook with fatigue and effort, yet neither had come close to winning.

Mrs. Cheney clapped her hands. "I do love a good contest."

"I do believe, Mrs. O'Leary," Mrs. Talmadge stated loudly enough for all to hear, "they're dueling over you."

"I'm not a prize to be won." Despite her flaring impatience with the suitors, she couldn't help but feel a bit flattered.

"Yes, you are." Luke's voice sounded tight, strained.

Her heart thrilled...even if was debasing and embarrassing to watch these two fight over her.

"Finlay." Gus grunted. "She's mine."

"I am my own woman," she reminded them. "Out. Go. *Now.*"

Neither paid her a moment's notice.

"Out!" She pointed at the door.

Mrs. Talmadge and Mrs. Cheney swung their faces toward her, scandalized.

Despite it all, Effie meant it—she wanted Gus and Luke gone from her shop. These two made a spectacle of themselves, embarrassed her in front of her customers, and blocked her sales counter. She couldn't even get to her ledger.

"Effie," Gus puffed, breathing hard, "I've nearly," another puff, "won."

"Take it outside." She meant it.

But the two showed no hesitation. If anything, they fought harder. Gus threw his body weight behind his arm and Luke's stance widened.

The muscle definition in Luke's back sharpened, outlined by clinging cotton.

"My money's on the marshal." Mrs. Cheney said to no one in particular.

"Me, too. Sorry, Luke." Mrs. Talmadge almost sounded contrite.

The ladies' voiced doubt in Luke's ability must have spurred him on, because he quickly gained ground. Luke forced Gus back, their locked arms hovering at a forty five-degree angle.

Gus grunted and fought back. Effie noted the cold determination in his eyes.

Luke leaned harder, his forward foot coming off the floor.

Effie's heart quickened as Luke tapped Gus's knuckles onto the counter.

Mrs. Talmadge hooted with delight. "I don't believe it— *Luke* won."

Gus swept his shirtsleeve over his soaked brow, muffling curses.

She might've called him on his language, but Luke snared her attention. In two long strides he'd reached her, grasped her shoulders, and kissed her soundly. He'd claimed his prize.

Seven

Over the next three days, the friendly competition deteriorated into warfare.

Luke found it amusing...and a challenge to best Gus at every turn.

Luke may have won the arm wrestle—by a hair's breadth, but Gus whopped his butt in a race to clear Effie's boardwalk of the twelve inches of snow that fell overnight.

Gus had relished the chance to get even.

Effie figuratively washed her hands of them, ignored the whole goings on. So she hadn't actually witnessed Luke's humiliation, which suited him fine.

Luke showed up first thing on Friday with a basket loaded with home-cooked delectable goodies for Effie's enjoyment; Gus took note and hightailed it to the bakery and the hotel restaurant, returning with more food than she could consume in the next two days.

Gus rounded up three talented seamstresses—why hadn't Luke thought of that?—and paid them to work the afternoon with Effie so she might catch up on her backlog. All Luke could do was volunteer to make deliveries, in town and to outlying ranches, though it took him away from Effie. It seemed they were back where they'd started—Gus in the shop with Effie and Luke on the road.

Luke heard a shipment was expected on the afternoon train, and rushed to the station to collect it before Gus could.

Luke delivered dirty laundry and collected Effie's fresh bundle from the widow she paid to do the weekly job. Meanwhile, Gus displayed his unnatural prowess in the tailor shop. That was something he couldn't compete with.

But on Saturday morning, Miranda went into labor...providing Luke with the perfect excuse to whisk Effie away from town on Sunday afternoon. She'd no doubt want to visit her friend and hold the new baby. Timing couldn't have been more perfect.

"He's beautiful." Effie smoothed a fingertip over the baby's satiny cheek as his eyes drifted shut. He lay snuggled in Effie's arms, bundled in layers of receiving blankets and a newly stitched quilt.

Late afternoon sunlight streamed through spotless windowpanes, casting the room in burnished gold. The bedroom hearth blazed, keeping the chill away. Outside, wind howled past, but could not invade the warmth and safety and love in this bedroom.

"Thank you." Miranda admired the gift she'd just opened—a dozen flannel diapers and several receiving blankets. "You've been so generous with us."

"You're my dearest friend. I'm told you can never have too many diapers or blankets."

Gratitude for the simple pleasure of holding this newborn babe swelled. It seemed to both fill an aching void within her and yet make that ache so much worse. A little button nose. A tiny mouth, slack in sleep. Hard to say who the babe looked like, yet, but Effie imagined she saw quite a bit of both Miranda and Hunter in their firstborn.

Effie pushed the rocking chair into gentle motion and turned her attention to Miranda. "How are *you* feeling?"

"Well enough." A quick smile lit her friend's face. She shifted in bed, propped up on what seemed to be a dozen pillows. "Tired, but well."

Effie shared a smile with her friend, one that resonated with happiness. "Have you decided on a name?"

"You'd think we played tug-o'-war, trying to name this child. I want Phillip after Dad, and Hunter's determined he have his own name. No grandfather's names and no Hunter, Jr."

"Any ideas?"

"Not yet."

Though ensconced in an upstairs bedroom, away from the high-traffic kitchen, noises of a full household filtered through the sturdy ranch house. Clatter of pans mingled with children's laughter. Heavy footfalls pounded up the stairs, apparently taking them two at a time.

Happy sounds. Family sounds. Though Effie enjoyed living in town where she was constantly surrounded by people, she found the commotion in this household to be so ever much better.

She wasn't so alone when the Finlays opened their doors and their home to her. She almost felt like one of them. They'd made her welcome on numerous occasions when the family gathered for holidays, Sunday dinners, and simply for the pleasure of good company.

No wonder Miranda had spent the last month of her confinement in her parents' home where she'd have the security of delivering with help of her mother and plenty of brothers to ride for the doctor when the time came. Now that she remained abed and healing from childbirth, she'd benefit from her mother's care.

"So." Miranda's expression carried a hint of mischief Effie knew so well. "Tell me all about the handsome U.S. Marshal who stepped off the train and kissed you senseless."

"How did you hear?" The answer was obvious—everyone in town already knew. "Never mind—of course you've heard. His name is Gus...and we were...friends...a long time ago."

"I hear his kiss in greeting went way beyond friendship." Her features lost their bright teasing. "Hunter told me you how frightened you were of this man. He said he—Gus?—had you backed against the wall."

How much could she possibly disclose? How much had Luke told his family? She wanted to believe he'd keep her shameful secrets to himself, but couldn't be sure.

"He caught me by surprise."

"Tell me everything."

This was her friend—a dear woman whose own romance, just a year ago, had cemented their friendship. If anyone would understand her reticence to accept a suit from either Gus or Luke, it would be Miranda...even if Luke happened to be her elder brother.

In truth, Miranda was in a unique position to help Effie shuffle through the conflicting emotions attached to both men. She trusted Miranda implicitly.

"Gus and I had a youthful romance, hidden and secretive." As she shared the highlights with Miranda, it became even more clear that the feelings associated with Gus were in the past. "Now, I've come to the frightening realization that there's no comparison between Gus and Luke. None at all."

Miranda's features softened with understanding. She reclined on the pillows. "The word about town is Gus has loved you since he was fifteen years old."

"So he says."

"I think it's romantic."

Effie chuckled, sharing a wicked smile with this dearest friend. "Until he showed up, unannounced, and with a predatory gleam in his storm-gray eyes, I'd not seen him in five years."

"Predatory gleam? I see why Hunter mistook your shock for fear."

"I *was* afraid." It was suddenly difficult to meet her friend's gaze. She'd surely give away too much. But she needed to talk and sort through the jumble of emotions, so in a low voice as to not be overheard, shared the dismal secret of her disastrous marriage, the fateful night in which she'd believed herself capable of murdering her husband, and flight from Hartford.

"How," Miranda asked, her expression filled with more surprise than disappointment, "did you manage to get away? It takes money, resources, time—"

"I saved every penny I could scrape together from the household accounts. Reuben couldn't be bothered with women's work, so he didn't notice a nickel here and three cents there. I also had a savings account I brought with me to the marriage, money I'd been given by my grandfathers. While it technically belonged to Reuben upon our marriage, he hadn't touched it—yet—and as the marriage deteriorated, I withdrew the funds and kept them secreted in a compartment in my writing desk."

"Oh, Effie." Miranda reached for her in a show of compassion.

Tears burned Effie's eyes as she grasped Miranda's hand. "It's over. It's been over a long while. You know the rest. I ran, far and distant, took a false surname and bought Pettingill's with my savings." She sighed, releasing Miranda. "Other than that, I vow everything I've told you is the truth."

She couldn't keep her attention on Miranda's face, not with tears filling her eyes, so she focused on the sleeping baby. "I told you my only salable skill was sewing, which was true. I didn't want to lie to you."

They fell silent, and Effie drew long, deep breaths, trying to settle the trembling in her body. Why was it so difficult to confess?

"And then Gus came for you." A bright smile had replaced Miranda's frown. "And kissed you senseless...and my brother found out and *he* had to make his intentions known."

Startled, Effie blurted, "You know? Did Noelle tell you?"

Miranda laughed. "In this household, no one has much privacy. Luke is as obvious as can be. He's been mooning over you for as long as anyone can remember, so no, Noelle didn't need to say a word. I do believe he took notice of you the moment you arrived in Mountain Home. Is it fun to have two handsome gentlemen vying for your attentions?"

"No. It's actually a good deal of trouble."

"I can imagine. I know my brother so well."

"The two men are locked in an ongoing competition, battling one another for me, as if I have no say in the matter."

"Luke is an exceptional man. Anyone would have a hard time measuring up to him."

"I'm realizing this."

Luke was a fine man and would make someone an exceptional husband—but that someone shouldn't be her. She wasn't so sure she'd make anyone a passable wife. She was more a divorcee, in the spirit of the law, than a widow. Everyone knew women who failed at marriage shouldn't be trusted a second time. Some moments, such as this, she found it inconceivable that one man—much less two—courted her with the intent of marriage.

"You're very deep in thought." Miranda hid a yawn behind her hand.

"I've overstayed my welcome."

"Oh, no you haven't. Who's the better candidate?"

"For marriage?"

"Yes. You might string the pair of them along for a long while, but eventually one of them will persuade you to see things his way. You'll have to choose."

And that was the heart of the matter, wasn't it? "I'm not stringing them along."

Miranda smiled with understanding. "If you don't mind my asking, which one do you want?"

"I don't know."

Miranda leaned forward, pressed a gentle, warm hand to Effie's knee in the manner of very close girlfriends. "You, my dear friend, are a horrible liar."

"Oh, I am, am I?"

"It's plain as day, written on your face. You're in love. Desperately in love...but I know you, and I doubt you're conflicted by divided loyalties. You're not in love with both."

Her heart rate took off like a runaway horse, galloping at full-speed.

In love? How was that possible? She didn't know what love was, had never been in love.

She was, however, infatuated with Luke. That malady had been coming on for a very long time, for more than a year, now. Snippets of images featuring him flashed through her mind. A captured memory of the expression in his eyes as he looked at her—*only* her—at the summertime church picnic. The touch of his hand at her elbow one springtime Sunday and the hint of a smile playing about his lips. He'd been so fully focused on her and her alone.

"I'm scared." Admitting that truth made her feel helpless, raw.

"Why?"

"I'm no good at this. I thought I loved Gus once, but that didn't last. My marriage was a disaster—I'm not capable of loving a man forever. I doubt I even know what love is."

Her friend gazed at her with compassion and understanding. A long moment passed, and Effie's trepidation grew. "When you're paired with the right man, it's easy."

Miranda spoke from experience—one year into marriage, she knew she'd made the best possible choice.

"How do I know if he's the right man?" How could anyone possibly know, until time proved it so?

Her heart thundered and dread tightened her chest. *Why* had she ever allowed herself to consider taking this risk? It would've been infinitely safer to hold fast to her resolution to remain unmarried. Safer, more certain...and significantly lonelier.

The baby yawned widely, screwed up his tiny features and cried pitifully. Miranda reached for her son and snuggled him close. The babe continued to fuss. "I had a hard time trusting Hunter. Remember?

Effie nodded.

"When I paused to examine my heart, what I truly felt inside, I knew. I *knew* he was the right man for me. I suspect you and Luke are meant for each other. He's known this for a year and a half—and I believe you'll come to know it, too."

Eight

The night of the Annual Children's Program, Luke came to the solemn conclusion that two marriage-minded men could *not* court the same woman.

Effie sat between Luke and Gus on a pew. Gus had the aisle seat, and a steady stream of well-wishers paraded past, made all sorts of excuses to say hello to Effie and to shake Gus's hand.

Gus must've jostled Effie from the other side, for her wide hat brim caught Luke in the cheek.

"Sorry," she mouthed, and they shared a secret smile—one bright spot in this ridiculous night.

Sheriff Talmadge came next in line to shake Gus's hand. Sandwiched together as they were, Luke couldn't help but overhear.

"It'll be mighty fine to have you in our office,

son." The sheriff pumped Gus's hand in a hearty shake. "Glad to make it permanent."

Permanent? Shoot. *Not* what Luke had in mind when he'd asked Talmadge to keep Gus busy.

"Thank you, sir."

"The Service will be sorry to lose you."

Gus chuckled. "I wired my resignation early this morning. They accepted, so I won't need to make the journey just to sign out."

From the pew behind them, Mrs. Whipple leaned forward between Effie and Gus. "Mrs. Abbott tells me you offered a generous sum for their home. Is it true?"

"Don't know how generous it was," Gus turned in his seat to better address Mrs. Whipple, "But we'll make it official in a few days when my wired funds arrive at the bank."

Dread slammed into Luke's gut with the speed of a locomotive. Gus, buying the finest house in Mountain Home?

"I know how long she's been talking about wanting to sell that big house. With their family grown and the stairs getting harder to navigate, she's been planning a house that's just right. No stairs. Small."

"Glad to be of assistance." Gus winked...apparently at Effie.

"Well, that's mighty fine news." Sheriff Talmadge grinned. "That's a lovely home, a lovely home indeed. And a short walk to the sheriff's office. And not far at all from Pettingill's."

Luke's thoughts reeled. How on earth could

he combat this latest assault? Gus, moving here, *permanently,* buying a big home meant for a wife and family. Mighty sure of himself, wasn't he?

Luke's guts twisted as he realized how much he didn't know. Had Effie given Gus reason to believe he had a chance? Luke had been around plenty in the past weeks, but no doubt Gus'd found opportunity to spend time alone with her.

Luke nudged her, and she glanced at him, clearly stunned by Gus's disclosures.

Whether that was good news or not, Luke couldn't decide. Maybe the stunned expression meant she was overjoyed at the thoughts of that grand house...and living there as Gus's wife.

Luke knew he must do something, *anything*, to compete..

Now Gus had Effie's complete attention and Luke didn't like it, not one bit.

"It'll be a fine thing indeed," the sheriff said, "to have you join our community. You've won the hearts of the people, saving Doc and all. They'll feel safe, with you on duty."

Mrs. Whipple gasped. "You saved Doc?"

Gus nodded. "His horse came trotting home this morning, past the sheriff's office, without him. I went to inspect and found Doc in the snow about three miles out. He'd called on the Nance family. Out cold, he was. I got him home."

"Doc woke up about halfway back to town," Talmadge said. "He's at home, resting. Likely be as good as new 'fore long, thanks to Gus."

"What do you think, Miss Effie?" Gus asked,

his expression a mixture of boyish hope and a confidence and certainty that made Luke seethe, "think you're gonna like having me around?"

She made a non-committal sound that could've meant anything from *possibly* to *I'm going to kill you as soon as no one's looking.* Luke wouldn't allow himself to read anything positive into her choked response.

Talmadge laughed. "Well, if she's not happy about it, there's at least a half-dozen marriageable young ladies who'll be happy to hear you're here to stay—my daughter among them. The ladies consider you quite a catch."

"I'm flattered." Gus dropped a meaty palm on Effie's knee. "But I've got my heart set on a certain young lady."

"*You,*" Effie stated, "are *not* talking about me."

Luke smiled at that her denial.

Gus chuckled. "Who else would I refer to, Sweetheart? Everyone knows I've been sweet on you nearly half my life."

The organ tapered off through closing notes, and Reverend Gilbert stood behind the podium.

Effie's posture stiffened. "Gus—"

The sheriff laughed and Gus joined in.

Were these men idiots?

Luke took Effie's hand and knew a moment's pleasure when she held on tight.

Folks hushed the talkers and Sheriff Talmadge waved goodbye and headed for his seat. Mrs. Whipple settled back into her place behind them.

Their amusement wasn't mean-spirited, or Luke would've been on his feet and hauling Gus outside—town hero or not.

Luke cringed as Gus snagged Effie's attention...and from Luke's vantage point, it seemed they shared a lengthy, private moment of earnest conversation.

Luke held Effie's hand and wished all the way to Monday he had her to himself.

How was he supposed to make that happen?

Through the first musical number by the children's choir, Luke mulled over the dizzying news.

He knew one thing as sure as shootin': Gus would hold on, keep fighting for her right up until she told him how it was going to be. Nothing Luke had done had convinced Gus to take his attentions elsewhere. No. If Luke were to have Effie to himself, *she'd* have to be the one to tell Gus to go.

First chance he got, he'd let Effie know things had to change.

The following afternoon, Effie left Noelle in charge and hurried to Murphy's Mercantile for groceries. She picked up a loaf of Whipple's Bakery bread, a one-pound bag of whole nuts, and four fresh oranges. She added several canned items to her order and had just paid when Luke entered the store.

She turned to him, a cheerful greeting dying on her lips. Something was *wrong*.

"Mrs. O'Leary." Luke's tone bit deep, like frostbite.

"What is it? What's wrong?"

"We need to talk."

Effie glanced back to the counter to find Mrs. Murphy watching them, listening with unabashed curiosity. Mr. Murphy had paused in his sweeping. The older man wiped a palm down his white grocer's apron and hadn't the good sense to look away. "I'll be back for my purchases momentarily."

She lifted the hood of her cloak as Luke opened the front door for her.

He followed on her heels. "Not at your shop. Noelle's there."

Of course. He wouldn't want an audience any more than she did. Where to go? She glanced both ways on Main, realizing every business would have people coming and going. They wouldn't find a warm, sheltered place for a conversation. And by the look on Luke's face, this conversation must happen now.

Without another word, Luke took her elbow and guided her toward her business. Before they reached it, he turned her down an alleyway between buildings and toward the empty lot behind. They passed her necessary standing in a copse of bare, snow-laden trees, and beyond into an empty, forested plot beyond. At least they were out of the way of prying eyes.

Luke halted and turned her toward him. His

expression was grim, but all menace had fled.

"You can't have both of us," he stated. "It's time to choose."

"I don't want you both." She blinked, blindsided, but yet she'd known it would come to this. The Annual Children's Program last night had been miserable for them all. She'd been a fool to think they could sit together as friends.

"I'm courting you, he's courting you, and I'm putting a stop to it. I realize you very well might choose him—it's a risk I'll have to take."

She'd never seen him so distressed. Tension constricted his voice and a prominent vein pulsed on his forehead. "Luke—"

"This morning, I purchased *this* property." His gaze bored into hers. "I bought it to build you a big, comfortable house, with convenient access to your shop. A house for *us*."

"I don't understand—"

He had her by both elbows. "Not two minutes later, what do I hear? Our illustrious town hero, August Rose the Magnificent, obtained a marriage license with *you* listed as bride."

"I did not agree to such a thing." Indignation flared. Did no one ask her what *she* wanted? First Gus and now Luke.

"Didn't ask you about that, did he?" Luke swore under his breath. "Never mind. Of course he didn't."

"This *isn't* a competition—I'm not a prize. *You* didn't ask me, either."

"To marry me? I most certainly did."

No, he hadn't—he'd told her he *intended* to court her at a leisurely pace and *one day*, when she was ready, he would ask. But that was an argument for another time. "You didn't ask me if I'd like to live here, this close to my shop. You just bought the property." Irritation made her sound petty, irritable, most unlike herself. She didn't like the woman she'd become under the pressure of courtship from two men.

"It was a Christmas present." His voice rose, startling a flock of birds from the bare branches overhead. They took flight and scattered. "I intended to slip the deed in your Christmas stocking on my parents' mantle, but Gus's marriage license derailed those plans. Word about is he's planning on a New Year's wedding."

She tried to pull away but he wouldn't let her go. She growled with frustration. "Will neither of you stop to consider I might want a say in my future?"

"Effie—" Shock registered on his features. "I did listen. You told me you want to stay here, in Mountain Home. You told me you love your business...so I figured out how we could make that work, how I could adapt my life to fit with yours."

His temper cooled, exposing heartrending sadness. "Are you planning to marry *him*?"

At this moment, she didn't want either of them. "No."

"Good." Without warning, Luke pulled her into his arms and nuzzled his mouth against her jaw and neck and scattering kisses.

She couldn't resist the pull of his warm, pliant mouth upon hers. He awoke a startling sense of *right*.

Is this what Miranda had meant? That she would know, with certainty, that Luke was the right man for her?

"I love you," he whispered against her ear. "I love you, Effie."

She stilled. She'd have thought his declaration would bring happiness, overwhelming warmth and completion, because she'd waited her entire life to hear those words. A great chill seemed to overtake her instead. She shivered.

He stilled, eased back, and held her gaze—a silent demand she confess the same.

She couldn't. How did one form those three words in that particular order? She'd never once told another soul that she loved them. Deep down, she doubted she knew the meaning of love. Never once had either parent expressed affection, not to each other and not to their children. Among the Scofields, it simply wasn't done.

During her youthful romance with Gus, they'd never uttered the words. Yes, she'd fancied herself in love with him, but now it was obvious she had not. Her infatuation had withered upon their separation.

She'd never been in love, and sincerely doubted she *could* be.

How could she lie about something so crucial to Luke, who *knew* what love was? To force those words, just to please him, seemed a greater betrayal than the lies she'd told upon arriving in Mountain Home.

Staring into Luke's heated gaze, she knew she couldn't say it, *wouldn't*.

He waited. As if he desperately needed to hear the words.

Resignation formed on his dear features, firming the set of his jaw, dimming the hopeful light in his eyes. He swallowed, his Adam's apple bobbing in the column of his throat. "We cannot go on like this. I *won't* go on like this. You must tell him you've chosen me."

That was no hardship. Her heart *had* already chosen. "I have. I've told him repeatedly."

He shook his head. "Telling him you will never marry again is not the same thing as telling him you've chosen *me*, that you will wed *me*."

Yes, she'd kissed Luke, *wanted* his affection and his kisses, and been moved by an undeniable connection between them. But it was all happening far too quickly. Without warning, her head swam and she feared she'd faint. *Had* she decided she would forfeit every freedom and marry Luke Finlay?

Her pulse pounded. What had happened to his gentle promises of patience? Hadn't he told her he'd wait until she was ready? But that was before Gus announced he would live in Mountain Home, spent far too much money on a grand house, and applied for a marriage license.

"You're right." She'd held Gus at bay with claims she'd never remarry—and her foolish choice to step into Luke's embrace the day he'd installed the new stove. But she'd not explained herself, hadn't told Gus how her heart had softened toward Luke. "There is a difference."

"Tell him."

He'd always looked at her with patience, compassion, as if the sun rose and set with her. Was it merely the marriage license and home purchase that triggered this lack of patience and compassion?

"I will. Soon."

She searched his face, alarmed at the coldness in his expression.

"When?"

"By Christmas—maybe after the holidays. I've tried to make him understand—and he couldn't—this might take time."

"You have until Christmas, Effie. Five days." He swallowed, his throat working even as his jaw clenched. "If you can't let him go, if you can't *choose* me, tell the world you've chosen *me*—" Emotion tinged his words with a bone-deep desperation that cut her to the quick. "We're through."

Nine

"Mrs. O'Leary—why, what brings you out in a snowstorm?" Mrs. Talmadge, a hen-breasted, middle-aged woman with kind eyes ushered Effie into her warm kitchen. The house smelled of spiced apples and buttery pastry, mingled with rich coffee.

"I'm looking for August Rose, or your husband. The Sheriff's office is vacant."

"Haven't you heard?" Mrs. Talmadge took Effie's cloak and bonnet and seated her near the warmth of the stove. "My man's in bed with a cough. Doc was here two nights ago, insisted he stay down."

"He's ill? I hadn't heard. I'm sorry—"

"Thank goodness that man of yours came—"

"He's not—" Effie interrupted, but it was no good. Mrs. Talmadge kept on as if Effie hadn't spoken.

"—to town when he did. Deputy Rose is out with a half-dozen riders, searching for that troublesome Erickson boy who ran off night before last. He's caused his mama more than her share of worry."

It all made sense now, why messages left at the boardinghouse—both verbal and written, as well as on the sheriff's desk—had gone unanswered.

Mrs. Talmadge set a steaming cup before Effie.

"August Rose is not my man." She stirred cream and sugar into her coffee.

"That's not what I heard tell."

"That's the problem—lots of talk going around, but it is inaccurate."

No wonder Luke had reacted so strongly to hearing about a marriage license on top of all the whispered bits of developing romance. He hadn't known what to believe.

Perhaps it was time to send a note to Luke. He deserved to know she'd made every reasonable attempt to locate Gus. Sooner or later, the trouble with the Erickson boy would pass, and Gus would go back to sitting at the sheriff's desk until Talmadge recovered and could hold down that post.

"It's not accurate? Whatever do you mean?"

"August and I are friends, that's all. I have no intention of wedding him."

"I hear tell he bought you the mayor's house.

And plans a New Year's wedding in that fancy parlor."

"It's news to me. I never agreed to either."

"Why ever not?" Mrs. Talmadge blinked, startled by the news. "Why would you walk away from a fairytale?"

She'd asked herself that question a half-dozen times since Luke issued his ultimatum. Her irritation and anger had passed, and now she saw the good sense behind it. "I don't love Gus. He's a good man and deserves better."

"Folks marry for good reasons all the time, often without love."

Effie savored the strong brew. "I've been down that road once, Mrs. Talmadge. I wouldn't recommend it."

"You're mourning awful long for a husband you didn't love."

Now that the Christmas rush was over, she have time to sew for herself. Perhaps the cornflower blue that just arrived. "I do believe my mourning period is coming to a close."

"That's good to hear. If you're not sweet on the deputy, maybe you have your eye on someone else."

"That I do. Perhaps you'll help spread a bit of accurate information."

"Oh?" A twinkle lit Mrs. Talmadge's eye. She no doubt remembered Luke and Gus arm wrestling in her shop. "Wouldn't be Luke Finlay, would it?"

Effie nodded.

"You've fallen in love. That must disappoint

Gus."

Her belly tingled with an anticipation and excitement. "I haven't had the chance tell Gus my heart is elsewhere."

Mrs. Talmadge *tsk-tsked.* "The young man will no doubt stop here to check in with the sheriff, and the minute he does, I'll make sure he knows you're waiting on him."

"There's my girl." Gus met her on the mayor's front porch. "Merry Christmas."

Gentle swells of festive piano music filtered through the residence. Laughter and muted conversation floated above it like a countermelody. The mayor's annual Christmas Eve party for the merchants and civil servants of Mountain Home was already in full swing.

"Happy Christmas. I'm glad you're finally back—I've been looking for you for days."

"I got your messages." He stepped too near. Warm lamplight spilled through lace curtains, casting patterned shadows on his features. "I've missed you, and it looks like you missed me, too."

"We need to talk." In moments, someone else would come up the walk, the door would open, and the host and hostess would expect them to enter. Now was as good a time as any to ensure he heard her decision.

If she waited until the evenings' festivities were over, Gus could easily come to an inaccurate conclusion. He'd no doubt expect to dance with her, sit with her at dinner, and escort her to the Christmas Eve service.

"Later. Let's get you inside where it's warm."

"What I must say won't take long."

"Come along. Not two minutes ago, Mrs. Abbott announced supper would be served shortly. Can't it wait?"

She held her ground. "Now."

He examined her expression. "Let's walk. Less chance of an interruption that way." He offered his arm, led her down the stairs and onto the paving stones that wound through flower beds, now barren and covered in snow. "In summer, I hear these gardens were exquisite. Mrs. Abbott's pride and joy."

He squeezed her hand where it lay in the crook of his elbow. Her other hand remained tucked in her muff. He gazed up at the house where lamps burned in nearly every window. Eaves dripping with wooden lace and winter's icicles. She saw this house through his eyes and all it represented.

"I bought this home for us." He cleared his throat. "For you."

"I've tried to explain, from the beginning, that I had no interest in remarrying. But I was wrong. I didn't explain myself well."

He cupped her face, searched her eyes. "Effie, if you're saying what I think you're saying, my answer is yes. It's always been yes."

"No. Wait." She tried to step back, but his

soothing caress held her fast. "I'm not the woman for you, August Rose, and I cannot marry you."

"Perhaps, in time..."

"No—and with good reason. These past weeks, I've realized my heart belongs to Luke."

She waited for the statement to sink in. Tinkling piano music carried from the house on a gust of frigid night air. In the dimness of the gardens, she couldn't make out his expression, but in her heart, she knew she'd wounded him...and it hurt.

"I want *you* to be happy, Gus, and find all your heart desires. I want you to find the perfect companion who'll love you for the man you are today, who'll be thrilled you came into her life—" her breath caught on a sob. "*I* deserve those good things, too."

"I *have* found that perfect companion, the one woman I want." His hands still framed her face. "I have you."

She shook her head in denial. He couldn't miss the gesture, not while cupping her head. "*I love Luke.*"

"I gave up everything for you," he whispered, so quickly, he may not have heard her heart-rending statement. "You said you wanted to remain in Mountain Home, so I uprooted myself and found employment here, for you." Emotion tightened his voice with deep, raw emotion. "I offered to return with you to Hartford so your sister could stand up with you in our wedding. At home, I purchased a diamond ring to put on your finger. I bought the best house in the valley, for you."

Why couldn't she love him back? *That* was what he asked. Every expensive, tangible gift was a gut-wrenching plea. He wanted her to love him.

And she didn't.

She *couldn't*.

Her heart belonged irrevocably to someone else.

Tears flowed freely over her cheeks. Shame washed through her and turned her stomach. How she regretted allowing things to get this far. She should've tried harder from the beginning to ensure he understood her. "I'm sorry, Gus. So terribly sorry."

"Then take pity on me. Marry me." He dropped to his knees on the icy paving stones. He pulled off her muff and swallowed both of her hands in his. His face turned up, catching just enough distant light to show intense and genuine desperation on his face. "I love you, Euphemia Scofield, enough for both of us. It's OK you don't love me back, not right now. I know I can win you. It'll just take time."

"Gus—" Obviously, he still had not *heard*.

"Unless you say yes, don't speak." He swallowed, a soft, audible thud. "Marry me out of pity. Marry me because I should have whisked you away from your father and saved you from Carmichael. We could've been blissfully happy."

He fell silent, kissed the back of her right hand, then her left. A hot tear upon her bare flesh signaled the depth of his distress.

How could she do this to him? She remembered that summer, how her young heart had broken when confronted with her father's fury. How desperately she'd missed Gus after Father sent him away.

But he'd come for her, across two thousand miles, because he loved her still.

She could understand his reasons, why he'd searched for her for nearly a year, why he'd resigned from a coveted post with the Marshals.

Ultimately, comprehending wasn't enough. In the darkest moment of the past four days without Luke, with his deadline ticking ever closer, she'd come to the stark, life-altering realization that Luke deserved better and Gus deserved better...and ultimately, so did she. *She*—Euphemia Carmichael—*deserved better*. Better than marriage to a man who loved her enough to move to Mountain Home and buy her the best available house. Better than marrying a man who loved her but she did not love in return. She deserved better.

"I'll make you happy," he vowed, his tone conveying the depth of his conviction. "I'll ask your opinion on every decision. I'll share every corner of my life with you. We'll have children, God willing. If you want to keep your business, then do it. Give me the dream I've sought for nearly ten years— you."

He reached deep into his trouser pocket and pulled something out...a ring. She saw it reflect in the long shadows from the house.

A more impassioned proposal, she'd never heard. But side-by-side, compared to Luke's simple declaration of love and his desperation to know she belonged to only him, Luke's touched her heart in a way she'd never thought possible, while Gus's saddened her.

"August." She tugged, urging him to stand.

He rose, that ring offered on the palm of his hand. Lamplight from the distant windows shimmered in his eyes as he held her gaze.

Her heart squeezed. "I've heard every word. Now hear me. I will marry Luke Finlay—not right away, and maybe not for months or even years. But I *will* marry Luke. I love him with the depth and breadth you've just voiced. Can you understand why I won't give that up?"

Slowly, as if swallowed in physical pain, Gus clenched a fist around that ring.

Agonizing seconds crept past.

At last, he answered. "Yes."

"Can you let me go now? Will you respect my choice?"

He tucked the fist containing his ring back into his pocket. "On one condition. Does he love you the way you deserve to be loved? Does he love you as much as I do?"

She considered the question, weighed it in her heart. She'd come to understand, sometime in these past four days without Luke, what setting a deadline had cost him. He'd known he might lose her—he'd said so himself. But he'd loved so much he'd been unable to share, unable to live another week without securing her promise and a brighter future. "He does."

"Forgive me," he said, "if I must assess that for myself."

Anticipation tingled through Luke as he made his way into the church for the Christmas Eve service. Yes, technically, he'd given Effie through tomorrow, but he couldn't help hoping she might come through the church's doors, search the crowd for his face, and join his extended family on their standard three pews.

He missed her with a bone-deep ache he couldn't shake.

Mrs. Gilbert, the reverend's wife, played *Silent Night* on the old organ. Heady scents of cinnamon and bees' wax candles brought to mind every Christmas of his past. Happy, joyful memories, centered around family and peace. Pine boughs decorated the caps of every pew, embellished with velvet ribbons and silver bells.

"Good to see you, neighbor." Hunter's father offered a handshake and warm smile.

"Merry Christmas, sir, ma'am." He nodded to Mrs. Kendall.

Right behind them came Hunter's older brother, Warren, with his wife and children. The church filled up as more and more folk left their rigs in the snowy yard and hurried inside.

Luke kept his attention on the door.

One of the little kids tugged on his sleeve. He glanced down to find his niece, Jessie. "Is Miss Effie coming?"

"I hope so."

His older brother, Del, heard what the little one said and glanced at Dallas. These two brothers evidently knew something he did not.

"What?" Their expressions told him he wouldn't like it.

"Nothin'." Del busied himself helping his little ones off with their coats and seeing them seated.

Mrs. Gilbert segued into *With Wondering Awe* and Luke's stomach dropped to the vicinity of his boots. "You know I'm waiting on Effie. If you know something I don't, now's the time to tell me."

Jessie squeezed his hand. "I'm sorry, Uncle Luke."

Mindful of her fancy curls, he resisted rubbing the crown of her head. Instead, he squeezed her hand. "It's OK, Jess."

Del seemed to debate the wisdom of sharing whatever was on his mind, but Dallas, far younger and apparently less concerned, met Luke's gaze. "We came into town early, right?"

Luke nodded—one sleigh left nearly an hour ago, as they'd agreed to drop off Christmas surprises for Hunter, who'd stayed home with Miranda and the baby.

"I don't think Effie's comin' tonight."

Luke's chest squeezed and he found himself clenching his jaw. He rubbed at the aching teeth with thumb and forefingers. He fought to keep his tone neutral. "Oh? Why not?"

Dallas split a glance between Luke and Del. "As we drove on past the mayor's place, we saw Gus down on his knees in plain sight, proposing marriage to Mrs. O'Leary."

Luke choked. His throat slammed shut and his heart seized in mid-rhythm.

Del clamped a hand on Dallas's shoulder. "Now we don't know that's what we saw."

The image burned on the inside of Luke's eyelids, and he hadn't been there.

"Don't know what else he would've been doin,' Del. He had both of her hands in his, kissed one and then the other."

"Thanks, Dallas." Del cut the boy off. "You've helped quite enough."

Ten

Effie came awake to a soft knock on her shop's front door.

She blinked against the sunlight streaming through her bedroom window's curtains. Fog muddied her thoughts and left her sluggish.

Christmas morning.

Quite possibly the lowest point in all her twenty-three years.

Luke's rejection still stung and tears threatened.

She'd gone in to the Abbotts' party only long enough to ask her hostess for paper and pencil, and the favor of delivering her note to Luke at church.

Please stop by—I've made the deadline.

She'd been intentionally vague, given Mrs. Abbott's penchant for gossip and the certainty she'd read it. She'd wanted the other woman to believe she'd completed an order to be picked up. But she'd fully believed Luke would understand and be eager to see her.

So *why* hadn't he come? It was the same question she'd debated much of the night, and it nagged her still.

In retrospect, she desperately wished she'd gone to Luke herself. She'd suffered an intense headache after the emotional exchange with Gus and wanted nothing more than to climb into bed and close her eyes. The thought of staying at the party and feigning joyfulness while Gus suffered was simply too much.

It had been a wretchedly long night and sleep had eluded her until mere hours ago.

She'd never felt so alone in her life. Not even when married to Reuben and isolated from her emotionally distant family.

The knock came again, more insistent this time.

She rolled over, snuggled deep beneath the warmth of the covers upon her bed. She rubbed her eyes and felt the grit of dried tears.

There wasn't a soul in Mountain Home she wanted to see. Not until she'd washed her face, put up her hair, and dressed properly.

Maybe she still wouldn't want to see anyone, even then.

She reached for the pocket watch she'd left on her bedside table. Ten-o'clock.

She sighed, yawned, and nestled in deeper.

Perhaps she'd stay in bed all day. No one expected her. After Luke ignored her invitation last night, she could not imagine he would call on her to spend the holiday with his family. Why would he?

She had no delusions Gus might want to see her, either.

She'd gotten exactly what she'd originally wanted. She was perfectly alone in the world.

She'd just tried on that wretched realization for size, looked at it from all angles in her mind's eye and berated herself soundly for thinking this would make her happy, when another knock sounded at her back door. Whoever had come calling at her shop's front door hadn't given up after all.

She decided to lay perfectly still and let whomever was there believe she'd gone out.

A minute passed, perhaps two.

The knock came again.

Maybe it was Luke. Her pulse leapt at the thought.

Of all her friends and acquaintances in Mountain Home, Luke was the most likely to seek her out today, Christmas day. *Maybe* he'd reconsidered.

No better day, ever, to seek forgiveness. Perhaps his heart would be softened because of the day's holiness.

Knowing she must look a fright, she slipped out of bed into the stark chill of her room, pushed her toes into waiting slippers, and donned her wrapper. She ran fingers through her snarled hair, gave up on trying to improve her appearance, and drew a breath for courage. "Yes?"

She'd raised her voice enough to be heard through the door—but whoever it was wasn't eager to respond.

"Who's there?"

Another gentle knock.

If this were Hartford, she'd think twice about opening the door. But this was Mountain Home and it was Christmas. She opened the door to a bright splash of morning sunlight and a rush of frigid air.

Her heart jumped at first glimpse of her visitor—Luke!—but no. A man, bundled up in a greatcoat—*Gus*.

His haggard appearance told her he'd passed as wretched a night as she. His usually jovial face had lost every trace of happiness, as if he'd aged ten years overnight. His luxurious curls were uncombed, tangled beneath his hat and his shoulders slumped with defeat.

She had done this to him.

Unfortunately, he seemed to see the worst in her, too. He tried to smile. "You look like death warmed over."

"I'd say the same about you, I'm afraid." She stepped back, opened the door wider. "Come inside before you catch your death."

He remained on the snow-packed path. She waited—maybe he would come in.

He watched her expression with such intensity it became more than uncomfortable.

"Why are you here?" she asked, just to break the silence.

He lifted a hand, offered a battered envelope. She'd not seen the once-white stationery clutched in his fist until he presented it. No street, no house number, no city. Just a name—her name—in her sister's painfully familiar hand.

"Merry Christmas, Effie." He gestured with the envelope once more, as if begging her to take it.

She reached for it, this letter from Tori. The younger sister she'd been as close to as Scofields knew how to be. They'd been estranged from the day of her marriage to Carmichael. When she'd fled Connecticut, she'd not dared notify her sister.

"How long have you carried this letter?"

"Since Reuben's death." He sounded exhausted, as if the flame had gone out in his soul. "I promised Tori I'd find you. I promised I'd give you her letter. Now I have."

He turned to go, his hands thrust into coat pockets.

"Why didn't you give this to me weeks ago?" Why *now?* Why give it to her at all, after their reunion turned sour?

He paused with his back to her. It seemed impossible he could wilt further, but he did. Several long seconds passed.

Effie shivered in the bitter cold. She folded her arms about her middle and rubbed her legs together beneath her too-thin nightgown and wrapper. She grew impatient waiting for Gus to answer.

"I didn't forget." He turned back. "Once I found you, I always intended to make Tori's letter a Christmas present from home. Unless we'd made it back to Hartford by now, that is. I'd have given it to you on the train."

She nodded.

"I want you to be happy." Gus met her gaze and she knew he spoke the truth. "That's all I want—for you to be happy. If that's without me—" emotion choked his voice, "then I'll learn to be OK."

"I'm sorry." She'd never been sorrier about anything in her life. If she could've loved him, could have been what he'd needed her to be, she would have. But love didn't work that way. Far too late, she thought she understood how love did work, what it felt like, and how badly love could hurt.

He shrugged.

She owed him a great deal more than an apology. She owed him gratitude and friendship—and those emotions rang true and sincere. "Thank you for your hard work to find me, to set me free. You were my only and my best friend while in my father's house. Until Mountain Home, you were my only friend."

"Yeah. Friends."

She hated herself for hurting him, for loving someone else.

Without another word, without a goodbye, he trudged away, heading aimlessly in the direction of the empty lot that now belonged to Luke Finlay.

Effie hadn't realized she could feel worse, more barren, more alone. But with Gus walking away, his head bent low against the wind and darkening skies, the flurries of snowflakes tumbling from the clouds like flour through a great sifter, Effie's breath snagged on a sob.

"Wait."

He paused but did not turn.

"Thank you." She fought to stabilize her emotion. "Thank you, Gus. Happy Christmas."

From the beginning, Luke had known either he or Gus would lose Effie. Simple mathematics. One woman, two men. They couldn't both win her.

He'd deluded himself into believing Gus would be the one to leave town, alone.

Until the past few wretched days, he'd not considered he might be the one on the outside while the pair happily celebrated their newfound, renewed love.

Christmas Day had never felt so bleak, hopeless, or lonely. This wasn't Christmas—not without Effie and not without the buoyant spirit of hope and gladness inherent to the season.

Surrounded by family and laughter, Luke's heart pined for Effie.

What on earth was I thinking, to give her an ultimatum?

Hunter noticed.

After the ordeal of the holiday breakfast,

Hunter pulled Luke aside in the only quiet place they could find in the crowded house—the barn.

Hunter got right to business. "Swallow your pride and go to her."

"Didn't you hear?" Luke shoved aside the mental image of Gus on both knees, proposing marriage. "August Rose proposed marriage to Effie last night in the mayor's gardens—make that *his* gardens...the house he bought for her."

"They're not married yet."

Luke shrugged. Effie had made her choice. Who was he to beg her to reconsider?

He fingered the tattered note she'd written him last night, beckoning him near so she might tell him, in person, of her engagement to August Rose.

He might be man enough to accept her decision, but he wasn't strong enough to look her in the eye and hear her apologize for choosing Gus.

"Have you seen her?" Hunter demanded. "No. You've heard the hearsay, that's it. For all you know, she refused him, and she misses you as desperately as you're pining for her."

Luke shook his head. "I heard he presented a diamond ring." Tears stung his eyes. He'd heard the happy chatter about the blessed event from too many who'd attended the mayor's party before church.

Luke figured Effie and Gus had spent a quiet Christmas Eve at the boardinghouse, sipping hot chocolate and planning their future.

"Do you *know* she accepted him?"

"I do." Luke withdrew Effie's final note and handed it over. "You're kicking a dead horse."

Hunter opened the folded paper and read its single line. Twice.

Luke shuffled the straw beneath his boots. "Nothing's going to change the facts. Gus won."

"That's what you got out of this message?"

"What else is there to understand?"

"Who gave this to you?"

"Mrs. Abbott."

"Her?" Hunter snorted. "That woman's a gossip. I figure Effie wanted to make this note sound like business, and she did a fine job of it. If Mrs. Abbott thought you were to stop by to collect an order, she wouldn't be all curious and talking about you to anyone who'd listen."

"Or maybe," Luke said, swallowing in an attempt to ease the tightness in his throat, "Effie planned to tell me she's accepted Gus's proposal. Forgive me if I don't have the strength to listen to that."

Once the annual family portrait had been taken in Mother's parlor, she bodily kicked Luke out of the house. "Go to her. *Go.* And don't come back until you've solved this. I can't abide your misery."

And to think he'd believed himself successful in hiding his grief.

Just proved what his mother had always

claimed—mommas have eyes in the backs of their heads. They know *everything*.

He'd go. Because mommas did know everything. And she was right.

He'd made himself miserable, and the only solution was to see Effie, even if it made things worse. At least then he'd know if his only option was to hire himself out. Somewhere. It didn't really matter where. It couldn't be here, not with Gus soon taking over as Sheriff and Effie, his wife, living in the mayor's former residence. Everything in this town reminded him of her.

His brothers were old enough now to take over the ranch, to do the work their father could no longer manage. If his worst fears were realized and Effie was forever lost to him, he would not stay in the valley he'd called home every day of his life.

It had been five days, two hours, and thirty five minutes—an eternity—since he'd pressured her with an ultimatum. If only he'd held his tongue and exercised patience, if only he'd followed through on his promise to court her slowly, none of this would've happened. True, he'd still be competing with Gus for Effie's affections...but he'd still have a chance.

Five solid days filled with regret, picturing her in the other man's arms.

Five wretchedly long days calling himself every name in the book.

He saddled up and turned toward town. Domino nickered and broke into a canter.

He felt like berating the gelding for looking

forward to this visit, but held his tongue. He'd done quite enough damage with words of late, and he intended to change that.

If Gus were less than a United States Marshal, town hero, *and* the community's beloved new Deputy Sheriff, Luke might be able to talk some sense into Effie. How could he complain? The man's worst offense was winning a lady's heart.

If Luke were magnanimous—which he wasn't—he'd admit Gus deserved Effie's love and affection. It might be a very long time before he could fake that level of benevolence.

His heart thudded dully in his chest, numb from the thrashing he'd taken over the past many days.

He slowed Domino to a walk on the icy streets of Mountain Home. Snow had fallen steadily since late morning, and it looked bad, like the weather could take another turn for the worse. He'd stable Domino at the livery, in hopes Effie would see him.

As Pettingill's came into view, the windows seemed dark. There was still enough light out she might not have lit a lamp.

Or perhaps she wasn't there. If not, he knew where to find her...with Gus.

Cold clear through, Luke dismounted and found the livery snug and warm, but not a soul about. The horses nickered in welcome as he brought Domino in from the weather, rubbed him down good and well, and saw to his water and feed.

When he could delay no longer, he stepped into the wind and driving snow and peered across the street at Pettingill's Taylor Shop...his heart pining for Effie.

One lamp was lit inside now. Good, she was home. He couldn't even consider the probability that she wasn't alone. If Gus was with her, Luke would say what he had to say, though Gus would hear every word. The man had a right to know Luke was desperately in love with his bride.

The shop's door was locked. He pounded on it, waited. With the wind whipping past, he couldn't hear movement inside. Had she left a lamp burning and gone out?

He knocked again.

Long moments slipped by and still nothing.

Despair, heavy and thick, suffocated him. He braced his forearm against the door frame and rested his forehead against it. His hat nudged loose, caught on the wind, and tumbled end over end, far beyond his reach.

Like Effie.

He couldn't muster the energy to go after it. It was just a hat. Without Effie, what did the loss of his best hat matter?

She was probably at the boarding house, sitting before a flickering fire in Mrs. Ihnken's parlor, sipping mulled wine or spiced chocolate and singing carols with Gus and many others. The thought of going to her there seemed to require energy he didn't have, but he'd do it. He *had* to.

He'd pushed back, prepared to turn away when the door swung inward. *Effie.* In mourning black and a lamp held high.

He took in every curve and plane of her sweet face, the darkened hollows beneath her eyes. She wasn't smiling. The spark of happiness was missing in her vacant eyes.

She'd been crying. He could see that now in the puffiness and red-rimmed tender flesh about her blue, blue eyes.

Her gaze seemed to drink him in, to take in every scrap of information his expression betrayed.

A slow, sweet smile deepened the dimples in her cheeks. She still looked so sad, so world-weary, so threadbare in spirit. No one should be this unhappy on Christmas.

Before he thought it through, he'd taken two brisk steps toward her—to do what, he didn't know. But there he was, in her doorway, and all it would take was an arm's reach and he could touch her.

Heaven help him, he had to touch her, to pull her into his arms, to hold her close, to claim her and put this awful disagreement behind them.

He couldn't force his gaze away, couldn't look beyond her to see if Gus lurked in the shadows, where Luke wanted to be more than anywhere in the world.

She stepped back, and in a wordless gesture, invited him inside.

Eleven

Hesitant, more unsure than he'd been in his life, Luke entered the shop and closed the door.

Surely, if she'd accepted Gus's proposal, she shouldn't be this despondent. Or alone.

But that was zero guarantee she'd consider Luke's proposal, either.

He realized she clutched a worn envelope and sheet of stationery in her hand. "What's this?" Stupid question, but he had to start somewhere, and jumping in with *I'm miserable without you* didn't seem the place to begin.

She glanced at the letter. "It's from my sister."

The envelope looked like it'd been around the world and back. She must've received it some time ago.

"Gus brought it to me this morning. He didn't stay long—" The tightness in her voice conveyed the pain and misery she tried to hide.

Ah—it made sense. "Your sister didn't know where you were. No one did."

She sighed. "Happy Christmas to me."

"Is this why you're upset? The letter?"

"What?" Her gaze was unfocused. "No." She walked deeper into the shop and set the lamp on the counter.

A long moment stretched as he followed her every move, willing her to confide in him, willing her to want him in her life.

At last she spoke. "I'm shocked you're here. I thought—"

"I couldn't stay away." Without meaning to, he approached. He swallowed, his gaze drinking her in. "God, how I've missed you."

"I missed *you*." The lamplight illuminated tears gathering in her luminous eyes.

He didn't want to make her cry. But they couldn't go on like this. He had to know the truth, had to hear it directly from her.

"Word is Gus proposed. Again."

She shook her head, pressed her face into her hands. Her narrow shoulders shook with emotion that clawed at his shredded heart.

He wrapped his arms about her and pulled her in. There had been too much heartbreak. He could see how devastated she was, how torn, that her pain fairly ate her alive. He didn't want this for her.

He wanted her to be happy, to regain that spark and fire that drove her, made her the successful businesswoman, an independent widow who knew exactly what she wanted and how to get it.

With her cuddled against his chest and her face pressed to the hollow of his throat, he could almost believe they had a chance.

She eased back, pulled a hankie from her sleeve and dried her face. "You're cold. Come sit by the stove."

She turned away, carried the chair that belonged at her sewing machine close to the heat. He hung up his coat and accepted the stool he'd spent so many hours upon, reading to her as she worked. Then, she'd enjoyed his company and wanted him near.

"How did we get here, Effie?"

Her smile brimmed with sadness and she twisted her handkerchief in her hands.

"Forgive me," he murmured, "forgive me for doing exactly what I promised you I would not do. I pressed you for an answer, and that was wrong."

His heart thundered in his ears. This was the crucial turning point.

"There's nothing to forgive." She searched his face...for what, he didn't know. "You told me you would not share—that I had to choose. You told me you...love me."

He did love her, more than life, but figured she didn't want to hear it.

"I've never said those words to anyone. Not my parents, not my sister. Certainly never Carmichael. Not even Gus...before, when we were young."

"Never?" He leaned nearer, surprised. Expressing love for family members, in word and deed, was as natural to the Finlays as breathing. He couldn't remember a single day when he'd not heard family express a simple 'I love you' and known it to be true.

She shook her head.

He could imagine how difficult it would be for a person who'd never known how to express or show love to trust that words could communicate something so precious...or that they'd be received well.

He touched her jaw, invited her to turn to him. She did, finally, her blue eyes round and frightened, but hopeful, too. "I'm the one who must apologize. You gave me a beautiful gift—a promise of a home of my own, your love, a legitimate offer of marriage—I couldn't force words that weren't there...I could not lie, not to you."

"It's OK." It killed him to admit it, but it didn't matter that she couldn't love him in return.

Grief yawned wider within him. The dull pain behind his breastbone burned hotter. He'd lost her, because he'd demanded she choose, though he might have lost her anyway. She hadn't accepted Gus, either, but that was poor consolation.

He'd known from the beginning she liked her life the way it was, secure in its insularity. She did have three options, after all: with him, with Gus, or continue as she'd been.

"Don't say it." He swallowed against the

dryness in his throat. "I already know."

She blinked. Her lashes spiked with moisture. Her dimples deepened as she pursed her lips. Heaven help him, he'd miss her dimples. He'd miss her laughter and her smile. He'd miss *her*.

So he simply held her gaze, soaked in the image of her face, the color of her eyes so he could remember. Later and always.

This was why he had to leave the valley, go far enough away as to avoid hourly reminders of all he'd lost. No wonder Miranda had left home for so long after Warren broke her heart. He understood, completely.

Her delicate brows drew together in confusion. "I haven't seen you in five days, couldn't possibly have given anything away. How do you know? Who told you?"

"Your choice is evident, Effie. You've obviously refused Gus." Pain seared through his heart, followed with a rush of grief so intense, he didn't know if he'd survive it. "And you've refused me."

"That's what you think you know?" She shook her head with vehemence. "Must I spell this out?"

What was she saying? "I think you'd better."

"*Yes,* I refused Gus, every single time he mentioned a future with me. He's never been the man for me, and I've known that from the day of his arrival."

Luke scrubbed a palm over his face. "Any reason why you didn't just say so, weeks ago? It would've helped, immensely, had I known that."

He might have never issued the fatal ultimatum.

She shifted on her seat, turning to face him. "I knew, before you told me I must choose. My heart already had."

His pulse roared in his ears, but he thought he'd heard her right. He wanted to jump in, to demand clarification, praying she'd decided to take a chance on him.

"Maybe—" She drew a deep breath, straightened her posture, and held his gaze for an electrifying moment. "Maybe it's time."

"What are you saying?" He wanted to pull her to him, kiss her until she confessed to loving him, too.

"Maybe this Christmas, it's time to open my heart to possibilities."

"Effie—" It came out as a growl, almost like a warning. He hadn't meant it to.

"The possibilities," she echoed. "The possibility that maybe it'll be better, different, right. With you."

He hardly gave her time to finish. He surged to his feet, caught her in his arms. She giggled with such pure joy as he swept her around and around, her boots leaving the floor in a swish of wool and flannel.

His laughter melded with hers. "I heard you right—you said *with me?*"

She tightened her arms about his neck. "Yes."

"I love you, Effie O'Lear—Scofield, whoever you are. I love *you*."

He set her on her feet, grinning like a fool.

Just having her back in his arms made *all* the difference.

"I love you, Luke Finlay. I love you."

"You mean it? Earlier, you said you couldn't lie—"

"Oh, yes. I mean it." Her dimpled smile faded. "Forgive me, please? I didn't know what love was. How could I? You're the first, ever, to show me."

That confession humbled him, nearly brought him to his knees. "There's nothing to forgive."

He kissed her, meant for it to be a quick peck, just enough to silence her, to assure her in ways words could not that he had no intention of looking back...just forward, to the future. *Their* future.

The kiss took on a life of its own. She seemed to melt in his arms, lean into his embrace, return the fervor and awareness and love.

It was all the more sweeter for the last week's misery.

Effie. *His* Effie. In his arms again, right where he wanted her. "You love me?"

Poor Gus.

"I do."

"Any chance I can get you to say those words in front of Reverend Gilbert?"

She laughed, the sparkle of life and happiness back in the depths of her eyes.

"We can find him at home."

"Now, don't rush me. Besides, your family will want to be there."

"We made it to Miranda and Hunter's wedding with less than an hour's notice."

"That's true." Her smile deepened. "And your sister was married in her mourning black. I want a wedding dress."

"I know a talented tailor." He remembered her sister—on the distant east coast. "And I'm not the only one with family that might want to attend."

"I've already written to my sister. She merely wanted to know where I was, and I told her. We aren't close."

"That's sad."

"My home is here, my *family* is here. If you'll have me."

Luke dropped to one knee, determined to give her no room for doubt. He kissed the back of her left hand, then her right. "I love you, Effie. I love you more than you can understand."

She seemed to bubble over with joy.

"It's true—I love you so much I about died from grief this past week." He thought of Gus and his conscience twisted. "My life is with you. My future is with you."

Tears welled in her eyes and her smile widened.

But he wasn't done. "I don't have a diamond ring, but I do have a lot out back and the money to build you a modest home." He swallowed, nearly overcome with the joy of reuniting with this amazing woman. "Will you marry me, share your home, here, with me, until our house is built? Will you take my name?"

She tried to tamp down her smile. "That's

quite a list. Care to add anything?"

He noted the teasing glint in her eye. "I'm sure I'll think of something."

She pretended to consider, tapping a fingertip against her cheek. "No request to take your heart and safeguard it always?"

"Can't ask that, 'cause you already have it. You've had my heart from the beginning."

"I *will* safeguard it."

"Is that a yes?"

"It's a yes."

Effie snuggled next to Luke in the sleigh. Domino cantered toward home and the sleigh bells jingled merrily. Brilliant sunshine reflected off fresh snow, and she was gloriously content to savor Luke's nearness.

He glanced at her, his smile warming her clear through.

Miranda's advice had proved correct...when paired with the right man, it was easy to trust, easy to commit. In the full light of day, with the dark week of doubt behind her, she could see with utter clarity how much she wanted to join her life to Luke's.

She'd thought she'd hesitate to set a wedding date, anticipated she'd want a long engagement and time to prove to herself that Luke would remain constant in his affection through thick and thin.

Somehow, everything had changed. The depth of his love for her was far more tangible than the scars left behind by Carmichael.

"Your family will want to know when the wedding will be." She couldn't help but smile at him.

"They can ask." He shrugged. "I'll tell them we've not decided yet." He stole a quick kiss.

She pictured the familiar commotion in the Finlay home, setting the tables, mashing the potatoes, children's laughter. The house would smell of roasting beef and fresh yeast rolls—she'd been a guest at their table so many times in the past year and a half, returning there felt like going home.

Luke had accurately guessed his parents, upon hearing their happy news, would insist on gathering the family together to celebrate. Sure enough, he'd come for her that very next morning, prepared to wait as long as she needed to dress and ready herself. She'd met him at the door, prepared to go.

"You know my family, *our* family." Happiness radiated from his smile. "It seems to be tradition that we have brief engagements. Hunter and Miranda win that contest, but look at the others— Gerald married after a one-month engagement. Our parents after just three days. Don't let them rush you."

"I won't."

"They'll understand if we're planning on next Christmas." He seemed hesitant to look at her.

"A full year?"

"If that would help, sure. I just needed to know you're mine. Now that's settled, I promise, this time, to exercise patience."

He'd provided a perfect chance to tease him. She couldn't resist. "Christmastime? I'd had my heart set on a June wedding. Perhaps a year and a half from now."

His Adam's apple slid down his throat in a prolonged swallow. She tucked her lips between her teeth, fighting a smile. "June, 1901. Or maybe 1902."

He glanced at her then. "Lookin' to win the prize for the longest Finlay engagement on record? I can do that."

"Are you sure that's OK?" She tried to appear pensive. So far, he'd accepted her words at face value.

"I'm good with it. I'll have time to finish our house, furnish it, ranch another season for my parents."

She sighed. "That's a shame."

He slid her a glance. "How so?"

"I thought you'd be a little more anxious to put a wedding ring on my finger."

"You know I'd marry you today…if that's what you want. But I learned my lesson, Effie—I'm done with deadlines. They don't work out so well for us."

"So our wedding date is entirely up to me?"

He flicked the reins, urging Domino onward. He glanced at her, his expression revealing hesitancy to give her complete control…as if he feared she'd put him off for a decade. "Pretty much."

"June, 1905. Has quite a ring to it, hasn't it?"

"Woman, you'd best be joshing me."

She chuckled, so filled with joy, she couldn't contain it. "In all seriousness, I want to marry you on New Year's Day."

"What year?"

"This one. In six days."

"I thought you wanted to make a fancy wedding dress."

"A dress doesn't matter," she told him, meaning it. "I've had a change of heart...I want marriage, to you. You're the right man for me. New Year's Day is perfect...for our new beginning."

Two days after the family celebrated Luke and Effie's engagement, Luke determined to speak to Gus. He well knew the pain the other man suffered. The wedding would occur in four days...and if he'd not yet heard, Gus deserved to know. The sooner something was said to clear the air, the better.

After all, Gus would be a lifelong neighbor. His purchase of the Abbott's house was complete, and just yesterday, Liam Talmadge had turned over the sheriff post to Gus. His cough had worsened, and he'd been thinking about retirement.

The sun shone bright overhead, reflecting mercilessly off the snow. In the street, sleigh runners and hooves had churned the slush to a darkened mess.

Luke stomped off his boots and pushed through the sheriff's office door. The dim interior smelled of strong coffee, wood smoke, and damp wool.

Gus looked up as Luke entered, at home behind the sheriff's desk. Otherwise, the small office was empty. Good.

"Finlay." Gus rose, offered a hand across the wide expanse of the battered desk. It'd seen a scuffle or two in its years.

"Rose." Luke shook with just enough pressure and a whole lot of steady eye contact.

"What can I do for you?"

"Nothing official. Just came by to shake your hand and say hello." *And apologize. Somehow.*

"I hear congratulations are in order."

Luke cringed. But Gus didn't seem, superficially at least, all that heartbroken.

But Luke knew still waters ran deep and Gus had to be hurting. "Much obliged. My congratulations to you, on the purchase of your new home, the job—" he gestured at the sheriff's office, realizing it both looked and sounded pathetic. He wasn't just a neighbor...he was *the* man who'd derailed the future Gus had planned.

God, he knew what that felt like. "It's a fine town. Good people." *Even me. Can you see that?*

"Yes, it is." Gus poured a cup of coffee, offered it to Luke.

He accepted, and took the chair Gus indicated

with a wordless gesture.

Gus poured himself a cup and returned to his seat.

Scalding hot, the brew was strong and flavorful and just right.

Before Luke could swallow and wonder where to take the conversation from there, the giggle of young female voices outside caught his attention. The door opened with a flurry of woolen skirts and delicate footfalls and frigid air.

Two young fillies, Miss Talmadge and the youngest Miss Abbott, each carrying a basket over their arms. Though the contents were hidden beneath tea towels, it was evident they'd brought lunch to the new sheriff. Well, how 'bout that. As far as he knew, Talmadge never had a lunch basket delivered, even from his own daughter.

Both young ladies glanced at Luke but quickly turned their attention to Gus.

Luke smiled behind his coffee cup. He'd seen what happened when two men set their sights on the same lady. He didn't see this working out well for Miss Talmadge or Miss Abbott.

Gus seemed to enjoy the attention. The ladies unpacked their baskets, chattered about homemade preserves and a fresh slice of cake...and wouldn't he like to stop by for another slice this evening?

"Thank you, ladies." Gus stood, towering over both girls. He tried to usher them to the door, but found himself fenced in by two very determined women.

It took Gus five minutes and a few promises to pay them each a call to get them out the door.

Gus shut it firmly behind them.

"That was interesting." Luke set his empty coffee cup on the edge of Gus's desk. "I don't want to keep you from your lunch. Sure looks good."

Gus offered his hand again. "Good of you to stop by, Luke."

"Friends?" Luke pressed.

"Friends."

He turned to go.

"One thing," Gus asked, interrupting Luke's departure. "It's not easy getting the short straw." Gus chuckled morosely. "Never thought she'd choose you over me, but she did." His features hardened.

Luke decided to let him have his say.

"Do you love her?"

"I do."

"Enough?"

"More than enough. She's my center, my life. I knew it from the beginning."

Gus seemed to weigh the answer. "It wasn't enough that she loved you. I had to know that your love for her is pure, complete, and selfless."

Luke nodded, understanding the gravity of Gus's words. "I understand."

"Do you? *One* time, Luke Finlay, *one step* out of line, and you *will* answer to me."

It wasn't an idle threat, but at the same time, it wasn't a threat at all. It was simply the truth, the plain, unadorned truth.

If tables were turned, Luke didn't know if he'd have the strength to shake Gus's hand and accept his friendship. Gus was apparently the better man.

Luke nodded in response. He accepted Gus's terms—but it would never come to that. They both knew it. There were simply no words to express Luke's deep and abiding love for Effie.

She deserved the very best in him—and she'd get it.

Every day of their lives.

On Sunday, December 31, 1899, Luke and Effie's wedding was held promptly upon the conclusion of church. Every member of the Finlay family was in attendance, along with most of the community.

Effie noticed Gus wasn't among the worshipers, and she couldn't blame him. In his shoes, she didn't know that she'd have attended, either.

She wore the most impractical, if simple, gown of white. Her mother-in-law-to-be, along with Noelle and Gerald's and Del's wives, had insisted on sewing Effie's dress. She'd long felt accepted and loved by the Finalys, but this gift somehow pulled her deeper into the bosom of the family, expressed welcome and affection that taught her even more about familial love.

Just before the wedding began, she hugged Luke's mother tight. "Thank you, Mother Finlay."

Tears filled the beloved matron's eyes. "I love you—*we* love you, Effie. You're our daughter, now, through and through."

"I will be, in a few minutes."

"We claimed you long ago."

"Thank you."

"Ready?" Phil Finlay offered his arm.

"Yes." Tears swam in her eyes and she blinked them away.

Caroline lowered Effie's veil, arranged it just so.

Mrs. Gilbert coaxed the first chords from the organ, and everyone gathered rose to their feet.

At the front, Luke stood in his Sunday best, his attention riveted to her. Love shone on his face, pure, complete, and certain. The sheer veil did little to hamper her vision, which was good—she wanted to see everything.

The aisle had never seemed so long before. If she could dispense with this tradition of walking toward her husband-to-be, she would have. She couldn't become his wife soon enough.

Phil patted her hand, passed her off to his son. He lifted her veil and pressed a fatherly kiss to her forehead. Father Finlay had shown her more affection, more love, more inclusion in his family than her own father ever had.

How strange, the butterflies in her stomach, the newness of this celebration—as if it were her first wedding, her only wedding. In some ways, it was.

Luke's hands were so warm, so steady as he

held hers. His hazel eyes had never conveyed such love, such devotion. Oh, she'd definitely made the right choice.

Reverend Gilbert cleared his throat. The organ's last phrase tapered to a note Mrs. Gilbert seemed to hold infinitely too long.

But at last ceremony began that would unite her life to Luke's.

The Reverend recited familiar words, phrases, stated vows for bride and groom to repeat. It all passed with a surreal beauty she held close to her heart and wanted to remember. With good reason, she'd blotted out all remembrances of the ceremony that bound her to Reuben Carmichael.

When the time came, Luke slipped a slim gold band on her finger. He kissed his ring upon her hand.

Love for this good man provoked tears she couldn't fight back. She didn't want to cry—this was the most beautiful moment of her life. She'd remember it as the moment that good won over darkness, that Luke's love reclaimed her.

"Ladies and Gentlemen, I give you Mr. and Mrs. Luke Finlay."

Applause erupted, echoing in the high-ceilinged building, but Effie's full attention was on her husband. In the full sight of God and a their entire family, he took her in his arms and kissed her.

Twelve

September 1900

Effie Finlay had seen every stage of their new home's construction...from the exterior. Luke had insisted she wait to see the finished interior once fully furnished and everything was in its place. Today, he was finally ready to give her a tour.

He stood flush behind her, his arms around her thickening middle. In three months, their first baby would be born in this house—their home.

New construction—fresh paint, varnish, sawdust, new upholstery and carpets—filled her senses. She touched the blindfold he'd tied about her eyes. "Let me see."

"Not yet."

He walked her forward, positioned her just so.

"Now?"

"Now." He untied the flour sack dishtowel from about her head.

From where they stood, Effie caught her first glimpse of fully furnished parlor and dining room beyond. Wallpaper of cream harmonized with stained and varnished door frames. An upholstered sofa and two chairs in complementing shades of blue clustered before the hearth. Large windows let in the morning light. A dining room table and chairs—*beautiful*.

Her husband's hands settled on her upper arms.

It was all so much more than she'd expected. Yes, he'd told her he'd saved through the years, but this was all too much. Overwhelming in its appeal and everything it meant. In her mind's eye she could see their family gathered around that dining room table, or seated before the fireplace on cold winters nights. She heard the laughter of children and pitter-patter of little feet.

"Do you like it?"

"I *love* it."

She felt him relax and she rested her head against his shoulder. He palmed her growing belly and she savored his touch. She'd long known he doubted his ability to provide a house to compare with that of her youth and the mansion Gus had bought from the Abbotts. She'd finally convinced him, throughout the entire construction, that she didn't need or want a fancy house. Until Luke, she'd never known a *home*.

Their newlywed home, the single room at the back of her shop, was filled with more laughter and joy and love than she'd ever known before him. It didn't matter where they lived, so long as they were together.

"Ready to see the kitchen?"

He took her by the hand and led her into the modern room, outfitted with a beautifully crafted oak icebox and a pump at the sink. A table stood in the middle at a serviceable height. A big cook stove filled one corner, a shiny, new appliance she hadn't the vaguest idea how to use.

Luke had offered to hire a cook, and she'd readily accepted. He'd continued to support her decision to operate her tailor shop—and that freedom had increased her love for him.

"Let me show you the bedrooms."

He led her up the stairs, taking her first into the bedroom they would share. Tall windows set into two walls of this corner room let in autumn's clear light and offered a beautiful view of the mountains. A big bed dominated the center, its four posts standing tall and straight. A matching wardrobe and dressing table stood against opposite walls.

"It's lovely." The room felt inviting, welcoming. They'd welcome their child into the world, here. In this sunlit room, it was easy to picture their future. Years stretched ahead, each day beginning and ending in its comfort.

His smile grew. "Let me show you the nursery."

A well-crafted crib stood under the sloping roof between two dormer windows. The baby's bed was already made with sheets and blankets to match. She recognized Mother Finlay's handiwork and laughed in pleasure.

The rocking chair's cushions were covered in the same fabric, as were the curtains at the windows.

Overcome with pleasure in this room that aptly spoke of their future, she turned in her husband's arms and put her arms about his neck. "It's wonderful. Thank you."

His embrace warmed her clear through. His hands smoothed over her back and found their way to cup her face. "You're welcome. It pleases me that we can finally sleep in our new home tonight. I'll carry your things in—you're not to lift a thing."

She smiled in appreciation, rose on tiptoe, and kissed him. "You're an amazing man, Luke Finlay. I thank God every day he brought me you."

"How is it possible I love you more today than yesterday?"

"Because there's more of me to love?" She smoothed the pale yellow summer dress over her rounded belly.

He chuckled. "Yes, I love you more because you're the mother of my children. I love you because you bring out the best in me, make me want to be a better man. I love you as we have the kind of marriage I'd always counted on, but didn't know I'd find."

She knew what he meant...a marriage like his parents', a partnership, one filled with love that deepened through time. He'd brought her this...more than she'd ever dared imagine could be hers.

Tears filled her eyes with too much ease these days. He dragged the pad of his thumb over the wet trail on her cheek. He understood. She could see the depth of their connection in his gaze.

"My life began the day I met you." She'd told him this before, but now, she meant it more than ever.

"That's what a man loves to hear."

He lowered his head and kissed her with confidence and tenderness...like a man in love.

Please *share* this book with a friend.
Paperback books are easy to lend.

Please *recommend* this book.
Please share your thoughts on this book with friends.

Please post a *review*.
Reviews from readers make all the difference to those browsing and buying, as well as to writers. Please take a moment and leave an honest review. One short sentence will do.

To Review *Maybe This Christmas* Online:

One Quick Click =
one page links you to all review sites
(stores where you might have purchased this title, and exclusive review sites like Goodreads and BookBub).

Simply type in:

www.kristinholt.com/review-maybe-this-christmas

(not case-sensitive, but dashes/hyphens are required)

Or scan the QR code.

DEAR READER

What about Gus?

This book is not the end of August Rose's story.

THE
Marshal's
SURRENDER

Holidays in Mountain Home, Book 3

www.kristinholt.com/book-description-
the-marshals-surrender

(not case-sensitive, but
dashes/hyphens are required)

Or scan the QR code.

Note: throughout the rest of my Dear Reader section, all bold-face words or phrases are links in the kindle edition—and connect to a wealth of background and historical information. If you're interested, please visit

www.kristinholt.com/history-maybe-this-christmas *(or scan the QR code)*

to view this same content <u>with clickable links</u>.

My warmest thanks for reading **Maybe This Christmas**. I do hope you enjoyed watching Gus and Luke decide who would qualify for Effie... only to realize the widow wasn't interested in either man.

This title is book two in an ever-growing series: ***Holidays in Mountain Home***. You'll find Thanksgiving, Independence Day, Founder's Day—much more than Christmas. While writing some of the later titles in this series, I began creating a page on my website about each book. These Description Pages contain links to related blog articles (historical connections!), Pinterest Board link, Goodreads links (how did other readers review it?), "Add to your Goodreads TBR shelf" links, quick access to my new "One Quick Click" review page, and more. You'll find the **Book Description for *Maybe This Christmas* here**. Come see, and enjoy the extras!

You may have noticed that my characters in this novella use the word "OK". **What about "okay"?** When did that word begin common usage? Are you surprised to learn the term had been around for decades by the time of this story (end 1899).

Much about Effie was particularly fun to write. **Sewing was once a standard household skill** little girls were taught to manage from a very young age. By the late nineteenth century, women of means owned **sewing machines** to speed up the never-ending process of creating, altering, and mending the family's clothing. Many purchased **ready-made clothing** constructed in factories. The wealthy often hired seamstresses to come into the home and spend weeks fashioning a new wardrobe for the upcoming season (or event such as a wedding). **Dressmaker** shops and **tailor shops** featuring custom work remained popular throughout the century.

The **fashions of the 1890s**—such as **humongous leg-o'-mutton sleeves**—were normalizing (thank goodness) by 1900. With trends of the shrinking **bustle** and balloon sleeves nearly gone, simple and somewhat masculine styles took hold. In the final years of the nineteenth century, women's "day costumes" consisted of fitted jackets (only slightly puffy at the sleeve cap) or a simple shirtwaist and **"walking skirt"** (an A-line with markedly less **adornment and fussy gathers than previous decades**). All of this implies the 'woman' has enough money for a new **costume** or two.

I'm lucky to have had a mother who learned stellar **tailoring skills** from her grandmother (who was married not long after Luke and Effie, BTW). I've sewn everything from wedding dresses to baby christening gowns to men's button-down dress shirts (with plackets at the cuffs). I enjoyed researching the sewing methods of the day, asking my mother a bunch of questions about a treadle sewing machine (as she learned on her grandmother's **treadle** machine—in its place of honor beneath the bedroom window). Today's **pinking shears** (zig-zag scissors) are still used by tailors, the **"pinking iron"** of the late Victorian era was a different and strong visual image (at least for me), so allowing the implement to make an appearance in this novella seemed right. I enjoyed fashioning the scenes of Effie's actual sewing and garment construction, including the **sewing of button holes**—the scene wherein we first notice Noelle Finlay (Luke's little sister and Effie's employee) for more than her Christmas costume finishing touches she doesn't want to sew herself in *Home for Christmas*.

I'm looking forward to introducing you to Noelle in her own **POV (point of view)**. That means we'll examine the story through her eyes and ears and heart. She's a newborn in *This Noelle*, a young woman in trouble in *The Witching Eve*, and caught in much worse trouble in *The Marshal's Surrender*.

It might appear that Noelle has grabbed more than her fair share of the stage or book spines. I'd agree—but must clarify that *The Usurper* is bossy Gus Rose. He's not only wielded the **Halloween short story** out of me, he's convinced me that he and Noelle deserve much more of a love story than presented in *The Marshal's Surrender*. I'm not sure I agree with the **U.S. Marshal**, but the man is beyond persuasive. Once you've read the next novel, perhaps you might let me know if you agree with Gus (more books about Noelle and him) or me (their story is told).

I'd love to hear from you. Did you find a typo (or

five) that slipped past several rounds of eagle-eye proof-readers? Please email me! You're welcome to contact me through my web site (**KristinHolt.com/contact-kristin**) OR email me directly: **Kristin@KristinHolt.com** (correct spelling is essential to receive your note; Kristin is spelled with an i).

You're invited to visit my website page for the *Holidays in Mountain Home* **series** to explore related titles.

With warmest appreciation,

Kristin

In Chronological Order:

Courting Miss Cartwright (Rocky & Felicity), **1879**
Book 5, Founder's Day NOVELLA

This Noelle (Phil & Caroline), **1881**
Prequel: Book 0.5, Christmas NOVELLA

The Gunsmith's Bride (Morgan & Elizabeth), **1885**
Book 6, Independence Day NOVELLA

Unmistakably Yours (Hank & Jane, Oscar & Ina),
1887
Book 8, Thanksgiving NOVEL

Home for Christmas (Hunter & Miranda), **1898**
Book 1, Christmas NOVELLA

Maybe This Christmas (Luke & Effie), **1899**
Book 2, Christmas NOVELLA

The Witching Eve (Gus & Noelle), **1900**
Title 7, Halloween SHORT STORY

The Marshal's Surrender (Gus & Noelle), **1900**
Book 3, Christmas NOVEL

The Drifter's Proposal (Malloy & Adaline), **1900**
Book 4, Christmas NOVELLA

http://www.kristinholt.com/holidays-in-

mountain-home-series

P.S. to find my page:
www.kristinholt.com/holidays-in-mountain-home-series

more quickly, see:

http://bit.ly/2A754ZY
(case sensitive)

or scan this code:

Books by Kristin Holt

www.KristinHolt.com/books

And while you're there, please sign up for her newsletter. *Be the first to hear about new releases, sales, and subscriber-only extras.*

Learn more about Kristin Holt's Series:

THE HUSBAND-MAKER TRILOGY

PROSPERITY'S MAIL-ORDER BRIDES

SIX BRIDES FOR SIX GIDEONS

HOLIDAYS IN MOUNTAIN HOME

And **collaborative works**

USA TODAY Bestselling Author

KRISTIN HOLT

Hi! I'm Kristin Holt, *USA Today* bestselling author of Sweet Romances (G- and PG-rated) set in the Victorian American West.

While secular in nature, my titles are "Appropriate for All Audiences" and appeal to selective readers and fans of Christian and Inspirational historical romance.

I write frequent articles (or *view recent posts*

easily on my Home Page, www.KristinHolt.com, *scroll down*) about the **nineteenth century American west—every subject of possible interest to readers**, amateur historians, authors...as all of these tidbits surfaced while researching for my books. I also blog monthly at *Sweet Americana Sweethearts* and *Sweet Romance Reads.* You'll find links to my blog posts and a wealth of information on my website:

www.KristinHolt.com

I love to hear from readers! Please drop me a note:

www.KristinHolt.com/contact-kristin

(Kristin is e-free.)

Or find me on Facebook:

www.facebook.com/KristinHoltSweetVicto rianWesternRomance/ *(Kristin is e-free)*

You're invited to join a fantastic Facebook group for authors and readers of Western Historical Romances (of all heat levels), Pioneer Hearts.

www.Facebook.com/groups/pioneerhearts

Kristin

www.ingramcontent.com/pod-product-compliance
Lightning Source LLC
Chambersburg PA
CBHW060422130626
46555CB00005B/2181